# THE SILVER SPUR CAFE

# THE SILVER SPUR CAFE

CHINLE MILLER

Yellow Cat
PUBLISHING

Cover by Cary Cox

*For Maya*

# CONTENTS

# 1

Bud Shumway tipped his patio chair back a bit, allowing for a better view of the big watermelon float sitting in the driveway of the bungalow he and his wife, Wilma Jean, had purchased a few years back when they first moved to the little desert town of Green River, Utah.

As their Basset hound, Hoppie, tried to jump up into his lap, an action not well suited to the dog's short legs and long body, Bud nearly fell over backwards.

He managed to grab onto the patio table and thereby avert disaster, though it was touch and go for a minute, and he spilled some of his cold drink.

"Bad little dog, Hopalong," Bud said in a stern tone. "You're supposed to look before leaping."

Bud pulled the little dog up onto his lap. His tan khaki shirt was now sprinkled with the pink watermelon spritzer he'd been drinking, a treat from Wilma Jean's most recent shopping trip.

He was glad he hadn't dropped the cup the spritzer was in, as he knew it was one of Wilma Jean's favorites. It bore the words, *Not Your Usual Cup of Tea*. She'd bought it in a second-hand store on one of her junkets to the town of Price, an hour away, where one could buy items not available in Green River.

The weekly trips helped keep Bud's wife from getting too frustrated with living in the small town, and besides, nothing was open here on Sundays, which also happened to be her only day free from the responsibilities of her cafe (the Melon Rind) and bowling alley (Tumbleweed Bowl).

Hoppie settled in just in time for his little dachshund friend, Pierre, to decide he also wanted to sit in Bud's lap. Bud reached down and managed to pull the little black-and-tan miniature weiner dog up, and Pierre splayed his little legs out, deciding to lay on top of Hoppie, as it appeared to be more comfortable than the little bit of Bud's lap that was left.

Bud smiled, feeling a sense of satisfaction that he'd rarely felt when he was Sheriff of Emery County, not all that long ago. He was very appreciative of his position as manager of Krider Melon Farms, which meant he was really just in charge of keeping the old tractors going and overseeing an occasional hired hand to help with the weeding and irrigating—until harvest, that is, when things could get a bit challenging, and then he earned his keep.

But working for Professor Krider meant that having a day off was really a day off, not at all like when he'd been sheriff and was always on call.

Back then, his days off still involved something or other, as it seemed there was always something going on around town—even though it was usually things like old Mrs. Jensen calling in because someone's dog was watering her carrots, or the high-school principal calling after some teen on a dirt bike had taken a shortcut across the school's front lawn.

And even though there was always something going on, none of it ever seemed to amount to much, except maybe the time a bunch of French tourists had decided to shower in the car wash, au naturel.

Bud had gotten a half-dozen calls on that one, and he'd purposely taken his time investigating it just to see how many more calls he'd get. By the time he got there, he'd received a couple of dozen calls, and quite the crowd had formed.

Bud now grinned and kicked back again, forgetting he was a bit off center with the weight of the dogs, nearly tipping over again.

He sighed, thought about the watermelon float he was supposed to be working on, then reluctantly stood, gently dumping the sleeping dogs from his lap. Opening the kitchen door, he went into the house, limping, as his leg had gone to sleep.

He'd make himself a cup of java, then get to work on that float. It wasn't going anywhere, since he'd unhooked it from the old John Deere tractor, but he knew he was delaying the inevitable. Might as well get it done.

He gave each dog a Barkie Biscuit from the Scooby-Doo cookie jar on the counter and then started some coffee in the percolator pot, just as his phone rang.

"Yell-ow," he answered.

"Sheriff, we got a problem."

It was Bud's ex-deputy, Howie, who was now sheriff but seemed to think Bud was still in charge from the way he always called him sheriff.

Bud waited, knowing Howie would spill the beans only when he felt like it.

Finally, Howie said, "You still there?"

"Still here, Howie. What's going on?"

"Well, I knew having actors in town would mean trouble. After all, they're from New York."

"They're in town already?" Bud knew a Shakespearean troupe was coming to Green River, but he hadn't been sure of exactly when.

"Roger. A bunch just arrived on the train. Problem is, they just arrived in the wrong town."

"The wrong town? Where, Grand Junction?"

"No, way worse than that, Bud. Thompson Springs."

"But the train doesn't even stop there, Howie."

"You and I know that, Sheriff, but they don't. Seems they got the engineer to stop and let them off."

"Well, it used to stop there, so maybe one of them was confused."

"I'd say if they're actors, they're probably pretty much always confused. Those guys spend all their time memorizing lines, and I'd guess they have no idea what's really going on. Can you imagine being married to one of them? I can hear it now, 'Wherefore art thou, honey?' Or, when they put out the dog, 'Out, damned Spot,' even though the dog's named Rosco."

Howie paused to consider the scenario, then added, "It would drive me nuts. Anyway, Sheriff, they're stuck there at the Silver Spur Cafe, and Jackson the cook called me to come and get them. Seems they're causing a disturbance."

"A disturbance?"

"They're quoting Shakespeare and acting like typical big deal New York actors, and they're about to get rotten tomatoed. Seems the locals aren't big fans of the Bard."

"Any idea how many there are?"

"Locals? Gee, Sheriff, I dunno. I thought Thompson had maybe about fifty people or so."

Bud groaned silently. "No, Howie, how many actors. In the cafe," he added.

"Jackson said there were a half-dozen. That would be about six too many, in my opinion."

"Well, Howie, I would guess we should go get them. I'll meet you in a couple of minutes at your office and we'll take that almost new Toyota Land Cruiser Prof Krider helped you guys buy."

Howie sounded relieved. "Roger, and 10-4."

Bud grabbed a cup of coffee, dropped a couple of dollops of vanilla-bean ice cream from the freezer into it, then walked out the door and got into his old Toyota FJ40, heading for the office of the Emery County Sheriff.

Thompson Springs was only 20 miles away, so he figured he'd be back home soon and could get started on that watermelon float, no harm done.

His figuring would be wrong, he was soon to find out.

# 2

As he pulled out of the drive, Bud forgot the float was there and almost backed into it, sidetracked by Howie's call and also by trying to hold his coffee cup in one hand and steer with the other.

Bud sure didn't want to wreck the float, especially since he was the one supposed to be restoring it. It was the centerpiece of the town's Melon Days parade every September, when Green River celebrated the region's major industry—growing some of the sweetest watermelons in the country.

It had only been a few hours ago that Professor Krider had called him, asking him to take one of the Prof's old tractors down to the River Museum and hook up the float, since he'd been volunteered to refurbish it. Of course, it would be on his work time, so he was actually getting paid to do it, as the Prof was donating Bud's time to the city, the float's owner.

Bud thought it was pretty good to get to work on something fun for a change—it was a far cry from his five-year stint as sheriff, where the most fun he usually had was trying to smile as his constituents complained over coffee and donuts at the Chow Down.

He was happy to be helping out, especially since it was for the professor. Ever since Professor Krider had discovered the little town of Green River and bought a melon farm, he'd become a sort of town benefactor, always donating to some cause or another, though he preferred to do it anonymously, like the big donation he'd made while Bud was still sheriff so they could buy a new patrol vehicle. By now, if a donation was anonymous, everyone figured it was from Krider.

Bud pulled out onto King's Lane and headed for town, turning onto Long Street. He put his coffee in the cup holder and took a pipe from his shirt pocket, a fancy reddish brown Plumb Brier he'd somehow managed to find at the Green River thrift store. It was his latest attempt at disguising what seemed to be a perpetual need to fiddle with something.

Bud had been a smoker and had quit when he'd met Wilma Jean, and he had no intention of taking up smoking again, but the pipe gave him something to do while on automatic pilot. He put it in his mouth and began chewing lightly on the stem.

It reminded him of pictures he'd seen of Mark Twain smoking a similar pipe, and even of Einstein himself. This made Bud feel like he was in good company—they must've been fiddlers, too, he thought, thinkers.

In fact, he was sure he'd seen a picture somewhere of Sherlock Holmes smoking a pipe, though now that he thought about it, it must have been a picture of someone playing the great detective, since Bud knew Sherlock hadn't been a real person.

And now Bud was one of them—brothers of the briar—even though he never put tobacco in his pipe. It was a brotherhood of intelligence, thoughtfulness, and stature, of favorite grandfathers and uncles, of aromatic smoke wafting on the breeze as philosophers shot the breeze over their pipes.

Bud smiled at the thought of a bunch of old geezers sitting around blowing smoke, and before he knew it, he was at the little ramshackle building that housed the Emery County Sheriff, though the sheriff himself was currently sitting outside in his green Land Cruiser with *Emery County Sheriff* on the door in bold black letters.

Howie was distractedly watching a car sitting at the drive-through window of the little drive-in across the street, called *Howie's* for its former proprietor.

Bud parked the FJ, stuck the pipe into his shirt pocket, quickly finished his cup of coffee, and got into the Land Cruiser with Howie.

"Morning, Sheriff," Bud said.

"Morning, Sheriff," Howie answered—then, remembering the numerous times Bud had reminded him that he, Howie, was the sheriff, corrected himself.

"I mean, morning, Bud. Say, you have any idea who's in that car over there? They look kind of suspicious."

"No idea, Howie. Why?"

"Why what?"

"Why do they look suspicious?"

"I dunno. The car's got Arizona plates, and the driver just looks suspicious, like he's checking everything out, like a spy. He came into the Melon Rind when I was over there earlier talking to Maureen, and now he's at my old drive-in, doing the same thing. He just ate at the Melon Rind, so he can't be hungry again already."

"Why are Arizona plates suspicious?"

"Because that's where the Superstition Mountains are, Bud, you know that."

"Howie, *superstitious* and *suspicious* aren't the same thing," Bud said.

"I know that, Sheriff," Howie replied, sounding somewhat irritated. "It's just that lots of suspicious things have come out of the Superstitions. Everyone's heard of the Lost Dutchman Mine, but you ever hear of the Peralta Mine? Spanish gold? Or Las Minas Sombreras? It's crazy some of the things that have gone on down there, and what goes on there doesn't necessarily stay there. It could end up right here."

"Howie, have you been reading those old lost treasure magazines again down at the office?"

Howie looked a bit guilty as he started the Land Cruiser. He replied, "Well, Sheriff, there just ain't much to do around here sometimes, and Old Man Green just donated a big stack to the library. I know I'm supposed to be working, but if there's no work to be done..."

His voice trailed off as he backed the Land Cruiser around and headed west toward the little town of Thompson Springs, while Bud again fiddled with his pipe, trying not to smile.

# 3

Bud and Howie were now cruising down the old abandoned highway from Green River to Thompson Springs, Howie dodging potholes like a Baja 1000 driver, going just a bit too fast, in Bud's opinion.

"Why not take the freeway?" Bud asked a bit nervously.

"I like the challenge here," replied Howie. "I figure I need the practice in case I ever have to chase some outlaw down an old abandoned back road full of potholes."

"Good thinking, pays to be prepared, and there's sure plenty of potholes around Green River," Bud answered. He then continued, hoping to divert Howie from speeding. "Say, Howie, I didn't know you wore jewelry. What's that bracelet you have there?"

The silver bracelet on Howie's wrist kind of reminded Bud of when he himself had worn a piece of jewelry, back when he'd had his ear pierced, or more accurately, when Wilma Jean had made him get his ear pierced.

It had been a ploy to make him quit fiddling, under the theory that if he had something embarrassing to fiddle with it would cure the habit. It obviously hadn't worked, so Bud had let the hole grow back together and instead taken up the pipe.

Howie, looking embarrassed, held his arm up so Bud could see it better.

"It's a gift from Maureen," he said.

"Very nice," Bud replied. "Your wife's a very thoughtful woman. What's those initials mean—what are they, *WWBD*?"

Howie suddenly dodged a big pothole, not even touching his brakes, as Bud grabbed onto the grab bar above his door. They drove on for a few minutes until Bud had given up on Howie answering his question. He noted a pair of antelope in the far distance with heads raised, alert, watching them.

Finally, Howie said, "It's Maureen's idea of progress. She says I call you too much for advice, and that I need to learn to go out on my own more. You know, make my own decisions."

Bud had noticed that Howie wasn't calling him quite as much as usual, though this simply meant the calls had gone from maybe a half-dozen a day to two or three.

"So, how does that work? I mean, a bracelet will help you make decisions?" Bud asked.

"This one will. See, the *WWBD* means *What Would Bud Do?* I'm supposed to ponder on that before I call you and see if I can figure out on my own what you would do and try not to bother you."

Howie looked a bit chagrined and added, "I know I call you way too much, but you have to remember I'm still a rookie. I'd been a deputy only a few months when you resigned and left me in this pickle."

Howie seemed a bit self-pitying, and Bud wondered if he'd forgotten how much he'd coveted Bud's job and how excited he was when Bud had left the force, if you could call a department of two any kind of force.

"See, Sheriff," Howie continued, "I was born really young and it takes me awhile to catch onto things other people find easy. By the way, what's that pink stuff all over your shirt?"

"Nothing. Just a little drink I spilled."

"Pink?"

"Watermelon spritzer."

"Homemade?"

"No, Wilma Jean bought it. Say, Howie, you have lunch yet? Maybe we could grab a bite at the cafe when we get there."

They were now on the outskirts of the little dusty railroad town of Thompson Springs.

"What about the Shakespeare actors?" Howie asked.

"They'll wait. They don't seem to be in a hurry to go anywhere. Where would they go anyway, even if they were?"

"Yeah, we can see if Jackson will make us a Hamlet and Cheese Omelet."

Bud laughed as Howie turned off the old highway onto Thompson Spring's main drag, its street sign long ago fallen down.

They continued a couple of blocks past old dilapidated buildings with broken windows, and soon pulled into the small parking lot of a bit less dilapidated building that had stood the test of time only because it was made of stone. A simple neon sign shaped like a giant cowboy boot with a spur read, *Silver Spur Cafe*.

Across the street stood a long brick building with a barely-legible sign that read, *Thompson Motel*. Its doors hung open, banging in the wind, tumbleweeds lodged in them as if trying to gain shelter from the elements.

A pair of railroad tracks ran right next to the cafe, and on the other side of them stood the abandoned railroad station with its sign, *Thompson Springs*. Bud figured the sign was probably there so travelers wouldn't mistake it for a real town in the night and accidentally get off.

In front of the cafe, a bright yellow four-door Jeep was parked askew, taking up several spaces. It had a sign on the door that read, *Cliff-Wrangler Jeep Rentals, Radium, Utah*, and its shininess seemed incongruent in front of the old cafe. Near it sat an old green pickup with oversized tires, probably for driving in the sand, Bud figured, though there wasn't much sand around Thompson, just clay.

Howie parked the Land Cruiser next to the Jeep and turned to Bud, asking, "Should I give him a ticket?"

Bud pointed to the bracelet. "What would Bud do?" he asked.

Howie looked disappointed as they got out of the Land Cruiser and walked up to the Silver Spur Cafe. Sitting around the corner of the cafe was a pile of trash—empty boxes and cans, an old tarp with holes in it, an assortment of bottles, and even an old dilapidated vacuum with a broken handle.

Howie stopped, looking at the junk, and said, "Man, if this was in Green River I'd have to give them a junk citation. Look, Bud, here's an old shovel, perfectly useable—I need one for those weeds by the office."

Howie picked up the shovel.

"And look here, an old container of radiator fluid, lid half off," Howie said with disgust as he picked it up and looked inside. "It's almost full. Someone's too lazy to throw it in the trash, and this stuff is bad if animals get into it. But I might be able to use it."

He turned and placed it and the shovel into the back of the Land Cruiser, then came back and looked inside the cafe door, trying to peer through the frosted glass to see if the actors were still there.

He then asked with consternation, "What if there's a big brawl going on in there between the locals and the actors? What should I do, Sheriff?"

Bud just shrugged his shoulders and pointed to the *WWBD* bracelet.

"Aw, c'mon. Bud, help me out here."

"Well, I don't hear anything, but Howie, the first thing a good lawman does in any situation is scope it out, assess it before acting."

"Right," Howie replied, gingerly opening the door and peering around the edge, Bud at his side.

"Looks clear to me," Bud whispered. "Let's go on in."

They both slipped in and sat down in the booth nearest the door.

The cafe's interior spoke of a better time in a lost past, the walls decorated with old photos that helped hide the peeling wallpaper.

The photos primarily featured old railroad scenes, with an occasional photo of an old-time cowboy or two, the real-deal kind that wore jeans with the cuffs rolled up and boots with the old-fashioned high heels that stayed well-anchored in the stirrups of saddles on half-wild horses. Mixed in were a few photos of wide-eyed people watching a train with what looked to be Teddy Roosevelt hanging off the rear car, waving an American flag.

Bud noted how quiet the cafe was, in spite of a group of a half-dozen people in nearby booths, a mix of men and women, all dressed in well-tailored suits that looked to Bud to be from about the 1960s. They looked as if they'd been mysteriously lifted from the heart of some business meeting in a city and dropped incongruently in the little cafe.

They were talking amongst themselves, but in a subdued manner, and it appeared to Bud that all was well. Whatever crises had prompted Jackson to call Howie had apparently been settled.

Bud kicked back in the booth and relaxed, pulling out his pipe, and Howie sighed in relief. No one acted like they'd even noticed them come in.

In a booth near Bud and Howie sat a couple, the man's back to them and the woman opposite him. Bud couldn't see her very well, but she looked pale-skinned with short red hair and was wearing what looked like a fake leopardskin coat and matching pillbox hat. Like the others, she appeared not only to be from the city, but also from a completely different era, and Bud guessed she was probably in costume for some media event or something.

Just then, the waitress emerged from the back kitchen and, noting Bud and Howie, quickly rushed over to their booth. She wore an apron over her blue jeans and denim shirt and looked to be in her mid-40s, her shoulder-length dishwater-blonde hair held back with a red and black polka-dot head band.

"Oh Lord, Sheriff," she said, her voice wavering. "I called for an ambulance from Radium, but it's too late."

Her voice broke, and she was barely able to whisper, "He's on the floor in the kitchen."

She started crying, then added, "Deader than a door nail."

# 4

The waitress collapsed into the booth next to Bud, her head on the table, sobbing, blocking him from getting up.

Just then, he could hear a siren, and an ambulance pulled up in front of the cafe, lights flashing. Two men and a woman jumped out and came running inside. They looked inquiringly at Bud, who sat looking helpless. Howie had jumped up, agitated, unsure of what to do.

Howie said, "In the kitchen," then looked to Bud for guidance, which wasn't forthcoming, as Bud was trying to gently get the waitress to move and not having any luck.

Howie fiddled for a second with his *WWBD* bracelet, then jumped up and followed the EMTs into the kitchen. He soon came back out with one of the EMTs and ran outside, then the two of them were quickly back, rolling a stretcher into the kitchen.

"I don't think whoever it was is dead," Bud said to the sobbing woman. "Because they wouldn't be hurrying like that. If they were dead, it wouldn't be so urgent."

The waitress now sat up and took the napkin Bud handed her, wiping her eyes. Bud noted she wore a name tag that said, "Penny."

She looked at Bud in disbelief, then jumped up and ran back into the kitchen.

In the meantime, the other cafe patrons were milling around, looking concerned but helpless. The man who had been sitting in the booth had stood, and Bud could see he was tall and thin and wore a perfectly-fitted and expensive blue-pinstriped suit, but like what the others wore, it was dated. He turned to Bud and asked, "What's going on here? Are you the sheriff?"

Bud replied, "I really don't know any more than you do. No, I'm the ex-sheriff, Bud Shumway." He stood and held out his hand, but the man ignored it.

"Well, it's sure causing us a lot of trouble. I hope they can get the problem solved soon. We're in the middle of an important discussion here. And you have something pink all over your shirt."

He then abruptly sat back down, his back again to Bud.

Now one of the other actors walked over to Bud and held out his hand, shaking Bud's. He was probably in his early 30s and looked like he might play Romeo if the troupe ever did Romeo and Juliet.

"I'm Julian, and I hope whoever is in trouble in there is OK." He rolled his eyes and nodded toward the man sitting in the booth, then said in a low voice, "Don't mind him, he's acting like an ass—problem is, it's not an act."

Just then, the EMTs emerged from the kitchen, Howie holding the door as they carried a man on the stretcher and out into the ambulance. The waitress followed, also getting into the ambulance, which took off, lights flashing and siren on.

Bud looked around for Howie, but he was gone. It appeared he'd also gotten into the ambulance, taking the keys to the Land Cruiser with him. He must have been really excited, Bud figured, and he sure hadn't consulted the *WWBD* bracelet, because Bud sure wouldn't have taken the keys.

Bud sat there for a moment, trying to figure out what had just happened. It appeared that he was now stranded at the Silver Spur Cafe in Thompson Springs, a good 20 miles from home, with a group of Shakespearean actors and possibly no one else to run the cafe. He suspected the man on the stretcher had been the cook, Jackson, and the waitress was also gone, as well as Howie.

Bud went back into the kitchen to further assess the situation. Yup, no one else around. He was on his own, and it appeared the cafe was abandoned, except for him and the actors. He looked carefully for any kind of clues as to what had just happened, but found nothing, no blood, no weapon, no sinister would-be murderer hiding in the bathroom.

As he went back into the main part of the cafe, he noted the tall thin man from the booth was standing at the cash register, looking impatient, tapping his fingers on the counter.

"I'd really like a check. I have more important things to do than stand in some rural dive waiting for my bill."

Bud noted the other actors were mimicking the man behind his back, making motions like a chicken would make if it could talk. It was becoming more and more apparent this man, whoever he was, wasn't well-liked, and Bud decided to just go with the flow.

He would to try to help out. "Let's see," he replied, punching numbers into the cash register, feeling pretty competent on that front, as he'd learned to run one while helping out Wilma Jean at the bowling alley and cafe. He had no idea what the man had ordered, but he decided to just wing it.

"That'll be $16.43, sir."

The man looked shocked. "For two cups of coffee? We didn't even get a refill!"

"Well, yes, I know that seems high, but you were drinking two cups of the finest coffee money can buy—Blue Mountain Jamaican. It grows in the world's most perfect climate for coffee and is closely regulated and very rare. It's hard to get way out here in the boonies, and we have to pay a lot more for it than most places. I trust that's not out of your budget?"

Bud was simply repeating what Wilma Jean had told him when she'd bought herself and Bud a pound of the expensive coffee off the Internet—it had cost plenty, and even though Bud didn't mind, she'd somehow felt the need to justify buying it, even though she was a major contributor to the family budget.

Now the actors were sniffling, trying to hold back their laughter.

"Of course it's not out of my budget," the man replied haughtily, handing Bud a fifty-dollar bill. "Keep the change."

Bud was a bit flabbergasted. He had no idea the man would take him seriously.

Bud said, "No, I'm joking, I don't even know what you ordered. In fact, I don't even work here. Being around you actors got to me for a minute." He tried to hand the fifty back.

The man ignored him and turned as the woman in the fake leopardskin coat grabbed onto his arm, and the pair walked out the door, getting into the yellow Jeep. The actors sitting at the counter broke into laughter, clapping and giving Bud high fives.

Bud checked the menu for the price of coffee, put enough in the drawer for their two cups, then placed the fifty-dollar bill in his pocket. He would return it to the man next time he saw him, assuming he ever did. He knew the man was somehow attached to the acting troupe, the way they'd acted like they knew him.

Now Bud wondered what to do next—maybe call the cafe's owner and tell them what had happened, although he had no idea who to call. For all he knew, the cook could also be the owner.

He was thinking about calling Wilma Jean when a van full of adults and kids pulled up, parking where the Jeep had been. It had Indiana plates and appeared to be a family on vacation, from the looks of all the tourist stickers on the side windows.

Bud looked around for a "Closed" sign, but didn't see one—but it was too late anyway, as the group was already coming in.

Just then, Julian the actor said, "We're waiting for a ride that's supposed to be coming. Any idea what could be going on?"

Bud groaned. He wasn't the only one stuck here, and he had a sinking feeling that things were about to get even more interesting, for now the gray car with Arizona plates had just pulled up, the same one they'd seen in front of Howie's drive-in back in Green River. A small man got out and started taking photos of his own car in front of the cafe.

Bud thought back to what Howie had said about the man being suspicious and wondered why anyone would want a photo of their car with the Silver Spur Cafe in the background.

## 5

The group from the van had seated themselves in two adjoining booths and were looking through the menu with relish, obviously looking forward to their meal. Bud hated to disappoint them, but he had no idea what else to do but tell them the cafe was closed.

This didn't sit well, and as everyone was digesting the news, one of the kids asked, "How can you be closed when you're open?"

It was a quandary Bud didn't feel he had the philosophical acuity to answer, so he said nothing. It seemed rather daunting to him to have to explain that someone had maybe almost died in the kitchen, and he wasn't sure what exactly had happened anyway. No point starting rumors, especially ones that had the potential of covering a lot of miles.

Bud thought of all the times he'd been hungry and come upon a restaurant, only to find it closed. He finally said, a bit lamely, "Well, if you don't order anything hard to cook, maybe I can do one last meal."

"Your last meal or ours?" asked the same kid, who Bud was beginning to think asked too many questions.

Bud replied, "Well, see, our cook is well, he's gone for the day. If you want something like a grilled cheese or a hamburger, we can do that, I think."

"What happened to him?" asked the same kid, who Bud now decided must be the spokesman for the group.

"I actually don't know," Bud replied. "I'll be back for your order in a minute."

Just then, the door opened, and in walked the man driving the gray car with the Arizona plates. He did kind of remind Bud of a gold prospector from the Superstitions, like Howie had mentioned, except for the fact that he looked a little too well-heeled with his expensive silver and turquoise watchband and matching bolo tie—but maybe he was a prospector who had made good. If he were a prospector, he wouldn't need much of a burro to carry him, as he was a pretty small guy, Bud noted.

Too bad Howie wasn't here to talk to him, Bud thought, because he really did look kind of suspicious. The man definitely was casing the place, looking around at everything with a very critical eye.

The man sat down in the same booth Bud and Howie had occupied a little earlier and picked up a menu. If Howie was right, this would be the guy's third meal of the day, and it was barely even lunch time yet. This reminded Bud that he still hadn't had lunch and was hungry.

He went over to the actors, explaining that he and Howie had been their ride, and how they were still stuck, himself included. He would call Wilma Jean when things slowed down for a moment and have her come get them all in her big pink Mary Kay Lincoln Continental.

Julian the actor got up and went to the door, and after figuring out how to lock it, pushed down on the lever. He then said to Bud, "Looks to me like it's time to close the cafe, but you're going to serve those folks, right? Let me help you out—I worked as a busboy in school. We'll take care of them, then we'll figure out what to do next."

Bud looked appreciatively as Julian walked over to the group to take their order. He had a strong almost uncontrollable urge to pull out his pipe, and was beginning to wish he'd been outside working on that watermelon float when Howie had called and had never heard the phone ring.

The man from Arizona had been taking it all in, and when Bud went over to take his order, he asked, "I saw an ambulance leaving here. Everything OK?"

Bud replied, "Not really. We lost our cook and waitress all at once. Not sure what's going on, but we're really short-handed."

The man replied generously, "I can help you out here. I've done plenty of cooking in my day. But I have to leave in an hour. I'll fix myself something in exchange."

Without further ado, the man got up and went into the kitchen, and Julian followed him with the order from the family.

Bud was shocked. A few minutes before, he'd been an innocent cafe patron, and now he was a restauranteur with his own cook and Romeo-looking waiter—plus a fifty-dollar bill in his pocket. You never know where life's going to take you next, he thought—kind of like a rodeo ride, silver spurs and all.

Not sure what to do next, Bud rummaged around a bit looking for a closed sign—there had to be one somewhere. Still not finding one, he decided to call Wilma Jean.

She didn't answer, and he got her voice mail, but he decided not to leave a message. There was no way he could explain everything, besides, he wasn't sure exactly what she could do to help at this point. He sat down in a booth and pulled out his pipe.

"Hey Mister, the sign says no smoking," the kid from the van yelled out.

"It's OK, I never light it," Bud yelled back, too discombobulated to explain further. He began chewing on the stem while polishing the bowl with his fingers, noting the fine texture of the wood. It seemed to help him think, and he was slowly regaining his composure when he noted another car pulling in.

Three older men got out and came to the door, trying to open it. They next peered through one of the big plate-glass windows, and seeing others inside, began pounding on the door.

Bud got up and unlocked it.

"Sorry, closed," he said.

"You can't be closed," replied one of the men, who Bud figured must be locals. "We have our Liars Club meeting here today."

"Say, you guys regulars here?" Bud asked. "Do you know who the owner is?"

"Yeah, it was old Tommy Gunther, but he died, as I'm sure you know."

"Died?"

"Well, yeah, he had a heart attack or something back there in the kitchen, not more than a couple of weeks ago. You the new manager? Where's the waitress, Penny? She was wanting the cafe, but she told me it's still in the estate or intestate or something. Can we come in?"

Bud opened the door. "Might as well," he answered. "Everybody else is here, well, except anybody who knows anything. Might as well add some good lies to the mix—that way we'll have both lies and confusion."

Just then, Julian came back out of the kitchen, and Bud decided to order a cheeseburger. He told Julian what he wanted just as his cell phone rang.

It was Howie again.

# 6

Howie sounded a little chagrined. "Gee, Sheriff, I'm really sorry, but I forgot to tell you there's an extra set of keys to the Land Cruiser up under the bumper in one of those hide-a-key thingies."

"Good. Good. Where are you, Howie?" Bud asked.

"I'm at the hospital in Radium."

"How's the cook?"

"I dunno. I haven't tried the cafeteria yet, but I am pretty hungry."

Bud sighed. "No, the one you rode in the ambulance with, Jackson."

"Well, I actually rode in the front with the driver. But not so good," Howie replied.

"What exactly happened to him?" Bud asked.

There was a long pause, and Bud could hear what sounded like a doctor's voice in the background on an intercom, saying something like, "Would whoever's bringing the cream-cheese cupcakes today please go to the front desk..."

Finally, Howie answered, "Cream-cheese cupcakes sound pretty good right now."

"What happened to the cook, Howie?" Bud repeated.

Bud waited until he thought the connection was lost, then Howie said, "I'm gettin' there Sheriff, be patient. I'm not sure. He had something happen in the kitchen there at the cafe, you know that, you were there."

Bud sighed, feeling that sense of futility that often plagued him when he was around Howie. "How are you going to get back up here?"

"I called Maureen, and she's gonna come get me. She wants to go shopping and have dinner at Smitty's Steak House. And there's a country-swing band playing out at the rodeo arena, so we thought we'd go to that and maybe get some band tips. Wilma Jean gave her the rest of the day off. I was calling to let you know about the keys. And don't worry, Sheriff, I'll have my phone in case anything happens needing me."

"Well, thanks, Howie, but see if you can find out more about the cook and what happened to him while you're there. Is Penny around?"

"She's back in his room. They won't let me in there, since I'm not family."

"Is Penny family?"

"Yeah, I guess they must be married or something, 'cause they let her go in."

Bud said, "OK, Howie, see what you can find out. I guess I'll close up the cafe and give the actors a ride to Green River, then head back home."

"OK, Sheriff, but they won't tell me nuthin', I already tried," said Howie.

"Can't you tell them it's official business? You're in uniform."

"I tried that, but they said it's in Radium County, not Emery, so I'd have to work with Sheriff Hum Stocks."

"But Howie, since it's closer to Green River, Emery County has an agreement to cover Thompson Springs. Did you tell them that?"

Howie was quiet. "No, I wasn't aware of that, Bud. This is the first time anything's happened in Thompson, that I know of, anyway. Nobody ever told me that."

Howie sounded sullen, and Bud could guess who he was thinking that "nobody" was.

"Well, try telling them that and see what you can find out."

"OK, 10-4, Sheriff. And Bud, you need to keep me in the loop on these things. We need a handbook or something."

As Howie was hanging up, Bud could hear him asking someone about cupcakes, so he figured he wasn't too upset.

Just then, Julian arrived with Bud's cheeseburger.

At first bite, Bud knew something was different with the burger, something different in a life-altering way. He chewed for a moment, then got up and got himself a glass of water.

After swishing some water around in his mouth for a bit, Bud took another bite. He wanted to be sure what he was tasting wasn't the taste of something else he'd eaten earlier combined with the burger.

Nope, it wasn't. The cheeseburger was definitely different. He closed his eyes and chewed slowly, savoring it. It was unlike any burger he'd ever had anywhere—truly transcendental, a perfect burger, more than the sum of its parts, with balance and finesse and...

Bud opened his eyes. He had momentarily forgotten where he was. He looked around, a bit embarrassed, even though no one seemed to notice, as everyone else was quietly eating their own burgers, maybe having their own transcendental experience.

Julian was over talking to his actor friends, and the guy from Arizona seemed to still be in the kitchen. The three old-timers were sitting in a corner booth drinking coffee and laughing.

Bud slowly came to himself, just as Julian walked over and asked, "So, any idea when we can get our ride?"

Bud replied, "Man, that's the best burger I've ever eaten."

He reverentially put the rest of the burger down, then said, "We can leave as soon as everyone clears out. This burger is to die for. But I'm curious, who was that guy in here with his woman friend? The ones who just left."

"That was Gregorio, our director."

"Director?" Bud was surprised. "You guys let him direct you even though you apparently don't much care for him?"

"Well, that's how directors are in general, disliked. See, actors are an independent lot and we hate being told what to do, yet part of our profession requires being told what to do. We live in a permanent state of cognitive dissonance. We're really a sorry bunch."

Bud grinned. "Sounds like a difficult life. Who was the woman with him? I don't mean to be nosy, but my wife's the one responsible for getting you guys this job, and she'll want to know everything— might as well tell me and save her from bugging you."

Julian replied, "Oh, that's cool. I'd like to meet her. We're all pretty excited to be here. It's way different for us, as I'm sure you can guess. The woman is Lucy, Gregorio's leading lady. She can be a bit dramatic, so be forewarned."

Bud took another bite of the burger, unable to resist, then mumbled, "Why is everyone so dressed up?"

Julian answered, "We just came from a production. Almost missed the train. No time to change. We had to ditch the audience."

"Shakespeare? In modern dress? Aren't you a Shakespearean troupe?"

"We are, but we do things a little different sometimes. It's our claim to fame. We just did a Vladimir Nabokov-type post-modern rendition of Romeo and Juliet. I was Romeo, but not the Romeo people expect, that's for sure. 'Tut, I have lost myself, I am not here. This is not Romeo, he's some other where.'"

Bud had no idea what he was talking about, but then, he was enjoying the burger, and thus somewhat distracted.

Finally, Bud asked, "Where did the yellow Jeep come from? Why didn't you guys just ride with what's his name, Gregorio, the director?"

"Oh, he rented it. The rental company brought it up from some town called Radium. As for riding with them, Gregorio told us we could just walk. Not so generous, but true to character."

"Where are you staying?"

"Some place called the Desert Star Hotel."

"In Green River?"

"I don't know. That's all he told us, was to go to the Desert Star."

Bud sighed. "The Desert Star is next door."

"No kidding? We've been sitting here waiting all this time when we could've just walked there?" Julian looked irritated, then added, "Well, that's what Gregorio said to do, walk. Problem with him is you never know if he's being an ass or being helpful. Usually an ass and seldom helpful."

Bud replied, "I don't understand how you're going to do a production in Green River when you're all staying in Thompson Springs."

"Oh, that's Gregorio for you. He thinks it's better to not mingle with the peons beforehand, and most everyone's a peon in his mind. The rest of the troupe will be in Green River. We're just the lead actors, so we'll stay here and go there for practice. I guess we'll ride in the Jeep, if he'll deign to give us a ride. Sometimes I wish I'd listened to my dad and become a dentist or something. But acting's my passion, for better or worse. I'm content to be a third-rate actor in a fourth-rate company, but Gregorio, he wants to be a famous director so bad it's killing him."

Julian stood for a moment, looking at Bud as if he wanted to add something, but thinking better of it, said goodbye, then went and rounded up his fellow actors. They all left, just as the tourists in the booth also got up to pay their bill.

"That was the best food we've ever had, mister," said the kid, smacking his lips as everyone else nodded their heads in agreement. "Kind of a religious experience, like in the Bible—you know, the Last Supper?"

The kid's mom pushed him out the door, smiling weakly, and the rest of the family followed, thanking Bud, who then locked the door and sat back down, eating the last few bites of his burger, lost in what Julian would probably call his passion.

Bud finished the burger, then finally found the "Closed" sign and hung it on the door, sighing in relief.

# 7

Bud had finally managed to get the Liar's Club to leave the cafe, and he was now locking up, as the actors were also gone. The man he now referred to as the *chef* instead of the *cook* had already left, probably when Bud was distracted, talking to Julian. He still had no idea who this chef guy from Arizona was.

Bud was wondering if maybe he wasn't some kind of mystery chef, like a mystery shopper, hired to go around to rival restaurants tasting their food and stealing recipes.

Problem was, the only restaurants in Green River were the Melon Rind and the Chow Down, and a more sophisticated customer would call neither a real restaurant, but just simple cafes. There was, of course, the Willows, but most people in town ate there only for special occasions, as it was expensive.

As far as Bud knew, neither of the two cafes used recipes for anything, and it was just scratch cooking. Kind of like chickens scratching in the dirt, the cooks scratched in the cupboard using whatever was available. Why anyone would want to check out their cooking was beyond him.

He found the hidden keys and fired up the Land Cruiser, heading onto the freeway ramp and west toward Green River. As he drove along, his thoughts returned to the actors he'd just met, then wandered on to the watermelon float awaiting his return.

Bud pulled out his pipe and stuck it in his mouth as he drove along, fiddling with it with one hand while driving with the other.

The town wanted the float (which usually sat in the parking lot of the River Museum) to look its best for its newest (and probably only) foray into haute culture—a phrase Bud had learned from Wilma Jean. He wondered why people used such phrases instead of just saying things in plain English. Maybe it made them feel educated or something.

Anyway, Wilma Jean had teamed up with the Prof to write the grant that had made this high culture possible, and it seemed fitting that Bud would be the one who ended up doing the actual physical labor part of the deal, fixing up the float that would serve as a back-drop to the stage where this so-called culture would take place, a stage which was really just the old flagstone square-dance platform down in the park.

Wilma Jean had filled him in just the other day—it seemed that every year the Utah Humanities Council appropriated funds to host a cultural event in places they considered culturally deprived, and this year, that place was Green River.

Bud had kind of taken umbrage when he'd heard that he and his fellow town folk were considered culturally deprived—didn't their annual Melon Days count for anything?

In fact, they'd had Howie and Maureen's country-swing band, Howie and the Ramblin' Road Rangers, play for the event last fall. They'd done a great job on some old Hank Williams' tunes, as well as some songs written by Howie himself.

Bud now thought of Howie taking the day off to go see a country-swing band down in Radium. Howie was making quite a reputation for himself, not necessarily at sheriffing, but rather, as the Singing Sheriff of Emery County.

Anyway, thought Bud, back on track. If haute culture didn't include things like old Hank Williams' songs, he didn't need no haute nothin', unless it was a haute dog or two.

Even though Green River had fewer than a thousand residents, there were big plans to entice tourists and nearby towns to the festival, which was going to be called "Shakespeare in the Sagebrush." The small Shakespearean company from New York was here to show the little town what culture really meant.

Bud wasn't too sure about the festival name, but he hadn't been on the naming committee. Seems like the Watermelon-Float-Fixing Committee was the only one he'd been asked to join, and he'd been elected chairman, secretary, and treasurer, all in one.

There was talk of the festival possibly becoming an annual event, one that the mayor had said would have the potential to put the town on the map, even though Bud knew it was already on the map, though you had to search for it a bit. It was right there in the middle of what Bud called the Big Empty, that big sweeping desert that was bounded on one side by the railroad tracks and by the scenic Bookcliffs on the other.

Bud kind of liked his little town as it was, but he knew more business would really help things out. Wilma Jean's cafe would get more customers, and maybe even a few would go bowling at Tumbleweed Bowl. And he knew Krider would sell more melons, which would indirectly help Bud, too. Maybe he'd even get a raise, though he was happy enough with how things were.

He now took the east Green River exit and was soon at the sheriff's office, where his old FJ40 sat exactly as he'd left it. He hid the keys to the Land Cruiser back under the bumper and was soon on his way over to the Melon Rind Cafe. He was wondering why Wilma Jean had never called him back, and he wanted to stop and make sure everything was OK.

Just then, his phone rang. It was Wilma Jean.

"Hi, hon, just calling you back. What's up?"

"Nothing much. You at the cafe? I'm almost there."

"Oh good. I need your help. I've been going nuts. I gave Maureen the rest of the day off, and we got busy all of a sudden." She paused, then added, "And hon, there's someone here you just *have* to meet."

Bud groaned. Working on the float was sounding better and

better as the day wore on. It looked like he was going to get stuck doing cafe work again, and he'd just quit his other cafe job, the one he hadn't even known he had until a couple of hours ago. Like Romeo and Juliet, he was beginning to feel doomed.

As he pulled into the parking lot of the Melon Rind, he suddenly felt even more doomed—there, taking up several spaces, sat Gregorio's yellow rental Jeep.

# 8

As Bud opened the door into the cafe, Wilma Jean made a motion for him to be quiet, and he could see she was standing next to a man in a booth, listening intently to what he was saying.

Bud recognized the back of the person's head, and he also recognized the pillbox hat that kind of floated above it, as if the man were wearing it, but which was actually on the head of the actress Julian had said was named Lucy and who was seated directly across from the man.

Bud also recognized the voice—Gregorio's.

"It's such a pleasure to meet the woman responsible for bringing us to our latest foray into theater, Shakespeare in the Sage."

It was a voice that grated on Bud, partially because he knew who it belonged to, and partially because he instantly recognized it as being schmoozy, which he resented. Schmoozing Wilma Jean was a position he reserved for himself, and himself only.

Now Wilma Jean corrected the voice, "Shakespeare in the Sagebrush, not Sage."

Gregorio continued, "No matter. 'What's in a name? That which we call a rose by any other name would smell as sweet.' But, dear lady, I tire of that quote, even if it is from our beloved Romeo and Juliet. There is so much more to the Bard than that rather simple play."

The director looked to Lucy for affirmation, and she quickly nodded her head in agreement, though it appeared to Bud she wasn't listening at all.

Bud quietly sat down in the booth catty-corner to them.

Gregorio continued, "It is my fondest desire to bring the Bard back to life via my directing, to communicate his mind and world to the audience in a fluid manner that pays testament to his talents—and to mine, I might add, humble as they are. Like Antonin Artaud, I believe that theater should be transformative, not just entertaining."

Now Wilma Jean's brow furrowed a little, and she asked, "What exactly does that mean? You're not going to do traditional Shakespeare?" She looked concerned.

*That's my girl. Can't pull the wool over Wilma Jean's eyes, and I should know that better than anyone,* Bud thought silently to himself.

Gregorio seemed oblivious. "Yes, we will be doing what you call traditional Shakespeare, but in a new non-traditional manner. You see, all art forms are ultimately connected. We will ask the audience to take a journey with us, a journey into a Shakespeare that even Shakespeare may not have been aware of, at least not on a conscious level."

He turned, and seeing Bud, asked, "Haven't we met? But please, a cup of coffee." He hesitated, then asked Wilma Jean, "You don't serve Blue Mountain Jamaican here, do you?"

"Hon, you don't mind getting him some coffee, do you?" asked Wilma Jean, turning to Bud. "Oh, Mr. Gregorio, this is my husband, Bud. We serve Folgers. Now, back to the play..."

Bud got up and returned with a cup of coffee, setting it in front of the director, who continued, now slowly sipping from the cup.

"Well, you see, we do experimental and experiential Shakespeare. We're going to ask the audience to participate, but in a meaningful way. It's my desire to turn the experience into a form of ritual that can be replicated in everyday life, yet ritual with meaning and texture. I will bring a taste of a different culture to everyone here, something that people who never get out of their ruts in your little town will find enriches their lives."

Wilma Jean now looked a little irritated. Bud watched intently. He was beginning to see trouble brewing, though Gregorio was oblivious.

"We will be tapping into a cutting edge culture, one with a very visceral feel that will put Shakespeare into the context of today's urban society. It's a new form, a new way of setting the Bard to music that's not really music..."

Wilma Jean interrupted. "Music? Shakespeare? What are you talking about? You're turning Shakespeare into a musical?"

Lucy of the pillbox hat now had a shocked look on her face, a look that said one never contradicts or asks questions of the esteemed director. Her eyes switched back and forth from Wilma Jean to Gregorio as if watching in horror as a rattlesnake was about to strike.

Gregorio seemed unperturbed. "Well, some would argue it's not real music, but is instead yet another more sycophantic art form. Hip-hop is a very visceral form and presents the world..."

Wilma Jean interrupted again, her voice rising. "Hip-hop? You're going to do Shakespeare to hip-hop? Isn't that the same thing as rap? I'm really not so sure Green River is ready for something like that..."

Now Gregorio looked irritated. Lucy had both hands braced on the edge of the table, looking like she was ready to bolt.

The director spoke slowly and firmly, like one would talk to a little kid. "I'm the director, and I decide what my troupe does. If you'll read the contract, it explicitly states that I have complete creative control."

Bud was enjoying this immensely, primarily because he knew who would win the contest. It was hard-won knowledge, won in the trenches of marriage. He kicked back and pulled out his pipe.

Wilma Jean said intently, "Well, Mr. Gregorio...say, what's your last name anyway?"

Gregorio acted surprised. "My last name?"

Lucy replied, "Anderson."

Gregorio shot her a look and said, "Andersoninski."

"And his name's really Greg," Lucy added, now sticking her tongue out at the director, which Bud thought made her look a little like a spunky Judy Garland in the old-fashioned hat. She had obviously broken rank and joined Wilma Jean.

Wilma Jean continued, her voice rising, "Well, Mr. Anderson-er-inski, I'm sure my friends at the Utah Humanities Council had no idea you were going to spring rap music on the unsuspecting citizens of Green River, or they would certainly not have contracted with you."

Wilma Jean's hands were on her hips, and the patrons in the cafe were now paying attention, patrons that Bud suspected were part of Gregorio's troupe, from the interest they were displaying.

"And you might like to know that we're really not the hicks you think we are. Many American towns have a long tradition of Shakespeare and still have Shakespearean festivals. Are you aware that there were many Shakespeare troupes throughout the Old West, many more than in England at that time? It was a major form of entertainment."

She paused, then added, "I'm willing to see what you come up with, but we actually contracted out a Shakespeare play, not a rap musical—Shakespeare in the brush, not in the hood. The folks in Green River are open to new art forms, but I'll be attending your rehearsals, and if they look like something that's not going to fly, we're going to have some serious talks."

She turned to go, then said, "And, sweetie, since you must be Italian with a name like Gregorio—though maybe your dad was Polish with a name like Andersoninski—you'll remember that old Italian saying, 'Once the game is over, the king and the pawn go back into the same box.'"

Wilma Jean disappeared into the kitchen, leaving Gregorio looking stunned, Lucy looking amused, and Bud trying to hide a grin behind his pipe, which try as hard as he might, he just couldn't help.

The director stood to go, and as he walked by, Bud tried to hand him the fifty-dollar bill from the coffee fiasco at the Silver Spur Cafe.

"You still have pink stuff all over your shirt," the director said, ignoring the money, then walked out the door, Lucy no longer trailing behind.

# 9

It was the next day, and Bud was home, kicking back again on the big porch, thinking about getting to work on that watermelon float, the dogs now sleeping at his feet instead of in his lap.

He was drinking iced tea from a tall glass that had a peacock feather embossed onto it in shades of green, blue, and purple, kind of reminiscent of something you'd see a movie star drinking from in some 1920s movie.

He was being particularly careful because Wilma Jean had forbidden him from ever touching it, as it was part of a vintage set she'd gotten in some antique store over in Grand Junction. It reminded her of her grandmother Frankie Jean, Wilma's partial namesake, who had been fond of the peacocks that hung around the family farm.

But all the dishes were dirty, so Bud had grabbed this one from the hutch while starting the dishwasher. Wilma Jean wouldn't be any the wiser, he thought, and he wouldn't let the dogs get on his lap just in case, so there wouldn't be any risk of dropping it.

His gaze now went to the watermelon float that sat exactly where it had been yesterday, before Howie had called and discombobulated Bud's plans. That float was one of a kind, and he knew that once he finished repainting it, it would really stand out as a backdrop to the Shakespearean play, assuming the production didn't get canned.

The float had been built on the bed of an old 1942 army truck, which had been detached from the cab. Someone had then welded a hitch onto the front of the rig. Old Man Green had donated it to the city when he heard they were trying to get a float going, and Bud had personally helped dig it out of the mud bog in Green's pasture, where he guessed it had been sitting since about 1944.

The float was made of plywood in a sort of watermelon shape, and kids would dare each other to ride in its splintery interior during the Watermelon Days parade, knowing full well they'd get in trouble if caught. It reminded Bud of the Trojan Horse he'd read about in high school.

The outsides of the float were painted to look like a giant slice of watermelon, seeds and all. Bud's job was to repaint it and then repack the bearings on the trailer, something he suspected hadn't been done since about 1942.

Bud finished the tea and set the glass down on the deck railing, distracted, pulling out his pipe and fiddling with it. He was now faced with what he considered somewhat of a moral dilemma, one with a difficult solution, if any.

The float had seeds painted on the watermelon, but his employer, Prof Krider, was now experimenting with growing seedless melons, the first in the area. Bud was considering painting the seeds out, but wasn't sure what Larry Digham would think.

Larry was Krider's main competitor and still grew the old-style melons with seeds. Bud badly wanted to show the world that Green River was a progressive kind of place, the kind of town that embraced change and seedless watermelons—and maybe even hip-hop—but he also didn't want to insult or antagonize anyone. He just couldn't decide what to do—leave the seeds or paint over them. It was a real quandary.

He'd get up and go to work on the float in a few minutes, he thought, but he was relishing having time alone to think, and he knew he had to solve this crisis before he could do much more on the float. Wilma Jean was down at the Melon Rind Cafe, and she wouldn't be home until evening.

Bud sighed, chewing on the pipe stem. He needed to get to work on that float, but the shade from the big cottonwood trees was so nice and cool, he was getting sleepy. He started daydreaming a bit.

Maybe he'd take up acting. He thought he might make a rather dashing MacBeth—but wait, wasn't MacBeth the one killed in the play? Or how about Romeo, even though Bud was a bit too old for the part, but he'd heard they could do wonders with makeup. But didn't Romeo also end up dead? He'd have to ask Julian.

This was the problem with Shakespeare, Bud thought, everybody ended up dead or wishing they were dead, and he suspected that those who wished they were dead were often the play's audience.

He had never really understood drama, as he himself liked rather lighthearted entertainment, like his favorite show, Scooby-Doo. Why would someone voluntarily go see stuff where people argued and were killed and the endings made them feel bad?

Bud stood, resigned to getting to work on the float. It was time to get busy. He took the dogs inside and made sure their water bowl was filled, then grabbed a sugar cookie from the Scooby-Doo cookie jar.

As he walked out the door, his phone rang. He could tell from the caller ID it was Howie. Bud stood for a moment, trying to decide what to do, then answered the phone, but he was too late. Howie had hung up.

Bud thought about calling Howie back, but decided if it were really important, Howie would call again. Besides, he had work to do.

He had made an important executive decision, and nothing was going to stop him from implementing it. He would paint each side of the float with just a few seeds here and there, but nothing very seedy looking, in what's called a diplomatic compromise.

Bud had no more than popped the lid on the paint can and stirred it when he saw Howie coming down the lane in his forest green Land Cruiser, police lights flashing.

# 10

Howie pulled up next to Bud, jumped out, and stood there like a tall lanky sheriff in an old-time Western, his hand over his gun, ready to draw.

"To shoot or not to shoot, that is the question," he said, grinning at Bud.

Bud replied, "Howie, cut that out. You're not shooting anything."

"I know that. I was just practicing."

"Practicing?"

"Yeah. I'm gonna be a star."

"A star? What kind of star? I thought you were already a country-swing star, or almost, anyway."

"An actor star, Bud."

"How's that going to work, Howie?"

"Well, see, Wilma Jean got me a job as an extra in the new Shakespeare production."

"Oh? What's the role?"

"I'm not sure yet, but that director fella, he was there in the Melon Rind when I stopped by to drop Maureen off, and they want me and her both to be extras. I tried to call you to tell you the news. I bet they'd hire you, too, if you wanted, even though you don't get paid. Say, what's this here in the grass?"

Howie picked up the peacock glass from where the wind had blown it off the deck railing.

Bud replied in dismay, "Oh, shoots, I forgot all about that. Is it broken?"

Howie held it up to the sun. "Wow, that's really pretty. Yup, it has a little crack on the rim. I bet this is something Wilma Jean bought and now you're gonna have heck to pay. Better get another one muy pronto, Sheriff." He sat it down on the edge of the float.

Bud groaned. "I don't know if that's possible, Howie. It's an antique."

"I bet you can find one on the Internet. But hey, need some help here? I'll help you get the float painted since you waste so much time helping me."

"That would be great, Howie. There's an extra brush there. Better put this old shirt on over your uniform, though."

Howie's uniform consisted of jeans and a khaki shirt with an emblem on the shoulder that read, *Emery County Sheriff*.

Howie was soon on the other side of the float, painting out part of the watermelon seeds, while Bud carefully painted out most of the ones on his side. Howie was talking to Bud the entire time, but Bud was only catching part of the conversation.

"What did you say about the play, Howie?" Bud asked, looking around the edge of the float.

"I said, they're going to do that play," Howie replied.

"What play?"

"I dunno. Everyone just says 'that play.'"

"Doesn't it have a name? Did Shakespeare forget to name it?"

"I dunno. Somebody said it's bad luck to mention it by name."

Bud stopped and thought for a moment. He could now guess what play they were doing—it had to be MacBeth. He didn't know much about Shakespeare, but he did recall his high-school teacher telling them about how the play was supposed to be cursed by the same witches Shakespeare had taken the spells from that he used in the play.

Bud dipped his brush back into the can of paint. It was amazing what one remembered from high school, probably not at all what the teacher had wanted him to remember, since it was about the only thing about Shakespeare he could recall.

"It's probably MacBeth," he told Howie.

"What about MacBeth?" Howie responded. "Somebody new here or something?"

"No, Howie, that's the name of the play. It's cursed, so you can't say the name or you'll be cursed."

"Looks like we're both cursed now, Bud," Howie replied.

"No, it applies only to when you're in the theater, though some actors won't ever say it. It's just superstition."

Howie had now come around to Bud's side of the float. "I'm going to be in a cursed play?" He asked with concern.

"Not unless you're superstitious, and that applies only if you say the name of the play while in the theater. Since you guys are doing it out in the open, I think you're OK."

Howie just stood there, looking concerned.

"I'm not sure I want Maureen in it."

"It's OK, Howie. It's just something someone came up with way back when people didn't understand things and were afraid of everything. It's not real."

"Kind of makes me think of that fella in the gray car we saw at Howie's—the guy from the Superstition Mountains."

"How do you know he's from the Superstition Mountains?"

"Because he's suspicious looking."

Bud groaned. "Did I tell you he came into the Silver Spur Cafe and ended up cooking the best cheeseburger I've ever had? Say, that reminds me, have you heard anything more about Jackson, the guy in the hospital? Were you able to look into that more?"

Howie was now back on the other side of the float. He yelled, "Yeah, Penny the waitress is back, and she told me he's still in critical condition. Man, thinking of the hospital, now I'm wanting cream-cheese cupcakes."

Bud sighed. "Any idea what happened?"

"She said he had a heart attack. I need to go see her and find out more. What do you think, Sheriff? I mean, that's the second heart attack there in the cafe in two weeks, and I'm wondering if maybe something fishy isn't going on."

"Well, Howie, things happen. Why would you think it might be fishy?"

"Well, old Jerry Gruber, you know him, he lives in Thompson and goes into the cafe all the time, belongs to this bunch they call the Liar's Club, a bunch of old geezers, he told me Penny's gone off the deep end. He was in the Melon Rind this morning, said he'd come to pick his wife up off the train. She's been visiting her sister up in Price, who has a daughter who just had a baby, guess it was a little boy and they named it after the grandpa..."

"Howie..." Bud interrupted.

"Sorry, Sheriff," Howie answered.

"It's OK. But what exactly makes him think Penny's gone off the deep end?"

"She dyed her hair down there in Radium, that's why."

"What's new about that? Women dye their hair all the time."

"She dyed it purple, Bud."

"Oh, that's different."

"Yeah," Howie continued. "And Jerry, he told me the Desert Star Hotel, you know, the one where the director and them are staying? Well, he said there's some guy who just bought it, and he's trying to sell shares in some new business he's starting, with the hotel as the main deal. He's turning the extra land there into an RV park and he's going to have campfire talks and horseback rides and all kinds of tourist things, take people up to see the Sego petroglyphs, that sort of thing. He thinks he's gonna make Thompson Springs into a big tourist trap."

Bud replied, "Well, good luck to him because he'll sure need it."

"Yeah," Howie continued. "And Jerry said this guy's been trying to buy up the Silver Spur and was mad at the old guy who owned it because he wouldn't sell it. That's the same guy who's now dead."

Bud carefully set his paint brush down. It was just like Howie to save the interesting information until late in the conversation, but this was pushing it, even for Howie, he thought.

"Howie, we really need to go talk to Penny."

"Why?" Howie asked, now back on Bud's side of the float.

"Because of all this stuff you just told me," Bud answered.

"You think Penny's involved in something bad? Rumor has it she wants the cafe."

"I have no idea," Bud replied, "But we should probably go see what she can tell us. Now that I have all this background info, two heart attacks in two weeks does seem kind of suspicious."

"That's exactly what I said, Sheriff," Howie reminded Bud a bit petulantly. "I need to call the Radium coroner and see if he did an autopsy on the cafe owner when he died. I figured that out from my *WWBD* bracelet. Pretty good, eh?"

Bud nodded in appreciation.

Howie added, "I'm done with my side. We can go to the Silver Spur when you're ready, 'cause there's nothing going on around town."

Just then, Howie's phone rang.

"Famous last words," said Bud.

# 11

Howie had left to go check out some problem at the hardware store, and Bud had finally finished packing the bearings on the float and was taking a break, kicked back in his big recliner in the living room, both dogs on his lap.

He had his laptop carefully balanced on Hoppie's head and was trying to find a new peacock glass on the Internet, but hadn't had any luck, especially since he'd gotten himself sidetracked reading a real estate ad he'd found for some place up in Wyoming. He wasn't really looking for real estate anywhere, but this ad had caught his eye.

*Priced for a quick sale! A fantastic property with room for a dairy cow with pen, a pig pen area, and a small waterfall within earshot of the master bedroom. Best of both worlds because no state income tax in Wyoming but Montana close by and Montana has no sales tax. This is not a typo, lock stock and barrel for $35k priced for a rush sale and will consider trade for silver or coins. Not only is this one of the most desired properties in this entire area, it's also an income producing property as it's a tree farm! This property produces about 100+ cottonwoods every year out of the grandfather tree's root stock. You simply dig them up, put them* *into pots, and sell them for $29.90 down along the highway. Serious inquiries only.*

Bud was trying to figure out in his head how many pots he'd have to sell to pay for the place, when he suddenly got a hankering for a dish Wilma Jean had made for dessert the previous evening—fresh strawberries with whipped cream on top.

What had made this really special was the fact that she'd put in a couple of tablespoons of orange-flavored honey as she was whipping the cream, and this had turned it into a real culinary treat. She told him she'd got the idea from some guy who'd come into the cafe.

Bud got up and went into the kitchen, taking out the electric egg beaters and whipping cream, as well as a tub of whipped orange honey a friend had brought them from up north in Honeyville, Utah.

He set to beating the cream in a big aluminum bowl—he wasn't sure if the bowl had some special properties or not, but since it was what Wilma Jean always used, he followed suit.

As he stood there, the beaters on high, he wondered about Penny and the Silver Spur Cafe and what could possibly be going on. Howie had promised to return when he'd settled the hardware store problem, but Bud figured they'd go talk to Penny another day—he was tired and wanted to rest.

He also wondered how things were going with the Shakespeare production. Wilma Jean was going to their first rehearsal down at the park this afternoon, so he knew he'd be getting an update on all that before long.

He noted the time on the the kitchen clock, the dog with the big eyes and clock on its tummy with a tail that moved as the clock ticked. Wilma Jean was due home before too long. He'd better get busy and get this cream whipped so he could eat dessert before she showed up and made dinner.

Now Hoppie and Pierre realized something was up in the kitchen and wagged their way in, Pierre eyeing Bud's pant leg and wondering if it would be fair game to latch onto it with Bud just standing there and not moving.

Bud was beginning to wonder why the cream wouldn't whip—it seemed like Wilma Jean never took this long. He put the beaters on super high and whipped some more, but it didn't seem like anything was happening, other than a little froth forming on top.

Finally, Bud turned the contraption off and got out a spoon, dipping it into the cream. Maybe there was something wrong with it, it was spoiled or something. But it tasted fine, it just wouldn't whip.

It was then he noticed the words on the carton: *Half and Half*.

Bud was suddenly very appreciative of Wilma Jean—without her, he would probably starve to death. He'd have to get her some flowers pretty soon.

He carefully poured the cream back into the carton, rinsed out the bowl, then stuck the spoon into the honey tub and ate a bite. He then gave the dogs each a Barkie Biscuit, unloaded the dishwasher, and went back into the living room and sat down again with his laptop.

He decided to check out the Salt Lake City news and see what was going on. The little town of Green River didn't have a newspaper, so about the only news anybody ever got about the town was from other residents. Bud liked to check occasionally and see what was going on at the state level.

As he scanned the news, he incredulously noticed an ad on the sidebar for the Desert Star Hotel. He clicked on it.

*Investors! Do you wish you'd been around to buy property near the national parks before they got famous? You know it! You'd be rich right now. Well, here's a once-in-a-lifetime chance to replicate that success, and this chance won't come around again, we can guarantee it!*

*Near THREE national parks is a sleepy little treasure, a town that sits on the freeway but that most don't even notice, yet it's right on the cusp of THREE national parks and poised to take off like hotcakes.*

*We're not going to tell you the name of this little town until you're ready to join us in creating a national treasure, one that will also fill your pockets with treasure because you got in on it at the right time. Right place, right time, as they say. You know it!*

*We have a secret, and for only $10,000 a share, you can get in on that
secret and help us build the West's next hotspot—and we're not talking
about Yellowstone, but good old Utah. We are incorporated, so you can't go
wrong. Join us!*

*Contact Zack Watson at 217-357-2989. (If you don't have $10,000 in
cash to remit promptly, please don't waste either of our valuable time and
resources.)*

Bud noted they mentioned the name of the hotel but not
Thompson Springs, but he figured it would be easy to find where it
was by searching for it on the Internet, which he tried. Sure enough,
the town of Thompson Springs came right up, first try. Some secret,
he thought.

He was now trying to figure out how many cottonwood pots he'd
have to sell to invest in the Desert Star Hotel when he saw Wilma
Jean's big pink Lincoln Continental driving down the lane.

He jumped up, glad to see she was home. He was curious to know
how the rehearsal had gone, plus she'd promised to make spaghetti
and meat balls for dinner, one of his favorites.

The dogs were now all excited, as they recognized the sound of
her car. Bud watched as she parked it by the old barn and got out,
wondering if he needed to help her get the groceries in.

It was then that his excitement began to fade—pulling up behind
her was a yellow Jeep, and a tall thin man with dark hair got out, and
even though he was now dressed in jeans, a plaid Western shirt, and
cowboy boots, Bud could tell it was Greg Anderson, AKA "Gregorio
Andersoninski."

Just then, Lucy got out of the passenger side. It took a minute to
recognize her in what looked to be Annie Oakley attire—a long
cowhide skirt with a fringe, a vest over a long-sleeved white shirt, a
Western scarf around her neck, and a lime-green cowgirl hat that
matched her lime-green cowgirl boots. Bud was wondering where
her six-shooters were, then figured she must be carrying a rifle
instead and had left it on the seat of the Jeep.

He couldn't believe his eyes, but it appeared his wife had invited the director and Lucy to dinner. He groaned and sank into his easy chair, pulling out his pipe, Pierre now deciding Bud was fair game after all, growling and chewing on his pant leg.

# 12

"I think dinner went pretty well last night, don't you, hon?" Wilma Jean asked Bud while putting a pot roast in the crock pot.

She added, "Turn this down to low before you go out to the farm, OK? It's for dinner—for the dogs. We're having salad tonight."

Bud groaned, hoping she wasn't on another health kick. The last one had about killed him off—Howie, too, as Wilma Jean and Maureen had conspired to make their husbands eat better and lose weight.

"Dinner went fine, considering who we had over," Bud answered. "Lucy's fine. But at least Greg finally let me give him back that fifty I owed him."

"What was that all about, anyway? And I know," Wilma Jean replied. "Greg can sure be a horse's ass, but Lucy's sure a sweetheart. I do think he's starting to tone it down some, though. Yesterday's rehearsal wasn't too bad."

"What's the prognosis on the play after one rehearsal?" Bud asked. "And the fifty was nothing, he just overpaid at the Silver Spur and I paid him back."

"Well, the jury's still out, but I do think it's pretty clever of him to have the actors all wear Western attire. He says it plays with the audience's preconceived notions—they're expecting Shakespearean costumes, and instead everyone's dressed like it's a Western. Then, to make things even more interesting, they do the lines as rap."

"Sounds like it would make things more confusing, if you ask me," Bud offered.

"Well, there's another rehearsal down at the park today, so come on down and see what you think. But I have to get down to the cafe. We're going to try something new today—cream-cheese cupcakes. Doesn't that sound good, hon?"

"We'll be having them with the salad?" Bud asked hopefully.

"Oh, I'll bring you a couple, but we won't make a habit of it. Howie got the idea from somebody, and Maureen's going to try out a new recipe."

She put on her jacket and turned to go, then turned back. "Say, hon?"

"Yeah?" he answered absent-mindedly, trying to solve the maze on the back of the cereal box while eating his Scooby-Doo cereal.

"Do you think what Greg was talking about last night is a good idea?"

"Not sure what you're thinking about," he replied. "He talked about a lot of stuff—in fact, he did all of the talking."

"You know, investing in that scheme in Thompson Springs?"

"I saw an ad for that in the Trib. Sounds a little shaky to me. Can you picture Thompson Springs as a tourist town?" Bud asked.

"Not in my wildest dreams," she replied. "I'm worried that Greg will buy into it, as he doesn't understand these little desert towns and their boom and bust cycles. And I've heard a few rumors about the guy running the hotel."

"Rumors? What kind of rumors?"

"Somebody told me he was good at marketing," replied Wilma Jean.

"I guess to some that would be a negative characteristic. I wonder what they base that on—not his ad on the Internet, I wouldn't think."

"I don't know. You know how people can be—anything different is questionable. I gotta run. Don't forget to turn down the crock pot."

Wilma Jean gave him a hug, then was gone.

Bud went outside and hooked up the watermelon float to the tractor and was ready to take it back down to the River Museum when his phone rang.

"Yell-ow," he answered.

"Hey, Sheriff," Howie said, "Any chance you can come to the rehearsal today? It starts at one. I can come get you if you want."

"I don't know, Howie," Bud replied. "I'm taking the float down to the museum as we speak, then I need to get the tractor back to the farm and start getting busy on some chores there. I've kind of been neglecting things."

The truth of the matter was, Bud was wanting some peace and quiet. Things were getting too hectic, and it was starting to remind him of when he'd been sheriff. He just wanted to go hang out on Krider's melon farm and enjoy the big cottonwoods and practice his bird calls. He needed to get the dogs out, too, as they'd been cooped up while he ran around.

He asked, "How'd things go yesterday, Howie? What was going on at the hardware store?"

"Well, I got there, and Wayne came out and said his Rug Doctor was missing and he just knew someone had stolen it. He'd unloaded it from Mrs. Simpson's car for her and left it sitting at the front door when someone asked him to show them the flower pots for sale out in the back. When he returned, it was gone."

Howie paused, and Bud could hear a train whistle in the background. He waited and was beginning to wonder if Howie had gotten sidetracked reading a *Lost Treasure* magazine or something, or even hopped the train, but finally Howie continued.

"Well, there goes Amtrak, late as usual. Anyway, that Rug Doctor theft sort of sounded like one of those buddy decoy deals to me—you know, where one guy decoys someone so his buddy can steal their stuff. And you know what, Sheriff? I didn't even have to call you. I just fiddled with my *WWBD* bracelet, kind of like you fiddle with stuff, and after a few minutes, the solution just came to me from nowhere, presto-insto. Pretty slick, eh? Sometimes I write songs like that, they just come from nowhere."

Bud decided not to comment. He asked, "What was the solution, Howie?"

"Well, I told Wayne I was going to fill out a report and then spread the word to all the locals to keep an eye out—if they noticed one of their neighbors had unusually clean carpets, they should call me. You know, law enforcement really should use citizen resources more—it would save a lot of time and money."

"No doubt, Howie," Bud agreed, climbing up on the tractor.

Howie continued. "But just as I was leaving, Wayne's assistant came over and told me he'd taken it inside, so it wasn't stolen after all. So that case was solved pretty fast, I have to say."

"Good work, Sheriff," Bud commended Howie. "You're doing a great job at keeping the town of Green River crime free."

"Then I spent the rest of the day at the Shakespeare rehearsal and then in the office."

"What did you think of MacBeth, Howie?" Bud asked.

"You're supposed to call it 'that Scottish play,' Bud," Howie replied with concern. "The director, that Gregorio guy, called it MacBeth during the rehearsal, and some of the actors got up and left."

"Just superstition, Howie. How did it go otherwise?"

Howie was silent, and Bud sat on the tractor, silently counting, one-thousand one, one-thousand two...

Bud's thoughts soon drifted to Penny dyeing her hair purple—they needed to go talk to her...one-thousand five, one-thousand six...

Howie finally said, "It was actually kind of weird, Sheriff. Not at all like I expected."

"Why not?"

"It's hard to explain. Sort of like a rap Western set to old-fashioned English or something. I could barely understand what was going on. In fact, I don't think I understood anything, to be honest."

"What part do you play?"

"Mostly I just stand around and look Western," Howie replied. "But I do get to be part of the rap chorus. We do this rap thing, drumming on whatever's nearby with our hands to help make noise—like this:"

Double double toil and trouble,
Pow, pa-pa-pow, pa-pa-pow-pow-pow,
Fire burn and cauldron bubble,
Pow, pa-pa-pow, pa-pa-pow-pow-pow.

"Pretty crazy, huh?"

Bud shook his head. "Seems pretty non-Shakespeare to me, but what do I know? Guess it's different, though."

He was now fidgeting with the tractor, ready to fire it up. He added, "I doubt if I'll make it, Howie, so carry on without me."

"OK, Sheriff. By the way, there's a stray cat hanging around the park. You guys looking to adopt one by any chance?"

"You'd have to ask Wilma Jean about that, Howie, I wouldn't know. We'd probably have to talk to Hoppie and Pierre and get their OK, too. Maybe you and Maureen need a pet."

"That's a thought. I'll ask her. OK, Bud. I'm on my way to get a cream-cheese cupcake, so 10-4 and pow, pa-pa-pow, pa-pa-pow-pow-pow."

"10-4, Howie. Keep on rappin' and stay out of trouble."

# 13

---

Bud had finished walking the irrigation ditch out by the big field to make sure the water was flowing freely. He and his helpers had burned the ditches in the spring in preparation for the growing season, and now that it was getting on into mid-summer, some of the weeds were growing back. He'd get one of the guys to bring a flame-thrower out here and clear a few patches that threatened to slow down the water.

He now surveyed the melons—they were doing great, and the new patch of experimental Israeli Galias looked especially hearty. He looked forward to tasting these, as last year's crop had been particularly sweet and had sold well at the melon stands.

If this year's crop was as good, he thought he might be able to sell them to a gourmet food market up in Salt Lake City, and if so, the farm would make a pretty good profit margin.

Bud loved Krider's farm, even though the professor was gone a lot to visit family in Texas—or maybe he loved it partly because of that. Professor Krider gave him free rein to run the farm as he saw fit, and Bud appreciated this freedom to experiment and try new things.

Maybe he was a bit like Gregorio, he mused, an innovator at

heart, though Bud's type of innovations were perhaps a little less radical.

Hoppie and Pierre were enjoying being outside, running in and out of the ditch water, and Bud knew he had to start devoting more of his time to his job, even though the weeding was about all that needed doing until the harvest. And even though the hired hand would help, he felt a little remorseful at not being out here more lately, especially since he and the dogs enjoyed it so much.

He sat down under a big cottonwood and pulled out his pipe. Hoppie and Pierre were soon at his side, shaking muddy water all over him and trying to sit on his lap.

"You guys are worse than me spilling watermelon spritzer," he said, noting his khaki shirt was now covered with mud spots. They settled down next to him, licking their paws while Bud fiddled with the pipe, thinking.

He was wondering why he'd been feeling so stressed the last few days—even though it seemed there was a lot going on, he knew he wasn't responsible for any of it.

The Shakespeare troupe didn't need any of his oversight, nor did things at the Silver Spur Cafe, though he was thinking of calling his good friend Hum, who was sheriff of Radium County, to see if he had any thoughts on the situation of everyone seemingly having heart attacks.

But Howie could just as easily look into that, and in fact, it was Howie's job, not Bud's. Bud had willingly and gladly left all that behind when he'd resigned as sheriff. So why was he now feeling stressed, just like he had when he was still in office?

Maybe it had something to do with that director fellow, as well as Wilma Jean being involved in it all. It seemed like the whole thought of a Shakespeare production was adding to the problem—maybe it was messing with his sense of who he was and what was familiar— his home culture and all that.

He picked up a shriveled-up melon that had been missed in last year's harvest, then took his pocket knife out and absent-mindedly began scraping off some of the peel, poking it down into the pipe bowl and tamping it down.

He now began thinking about Lucy, the actress that Julian had said was Gregorio's leading lady, wondering if that meant she was his leading lady in the play or was his leading lady in his life—or maybe both.

It didn't really make any difference to Bud either way, except he liked to study human behavior and had found it kind of odd that she'd been so in tune with the director in the Silver Spur and had then done an immediate turn about later in the Melon Rind when Wilma Jean had chewed Gregorio out.

But then, they'd both showed up for dinner, so whatever that was must have been ironed out, he figured.

Bud now fished around in his pocket for a lighter, then suddenly realized what he was doing.

He sat the pipe down. He had inadvertently reverted to his smoking days, just like that, without even thinking about it.

It was kind of scary, he thought, how easily he'd slipped into automatic pilot, especially after not smoking for so many years. He really was stressed—maybe even more so than he thought.

Thinking he should maybe find something a little less dangerous to fiddle with, Bud emptied the pipe and put it back into his pocket. The dogs were now fast asleep, Hoppie yipping and twitching like he was chasing a rabbit.

Bud himself was starting to feel sleepy, and he wondered if he ever twitched and yelped in his sleep—probably not, or Wilma Jean would've been sure to point it out, probably by kicking him out of bed.

He leaned back against the big cottonwood and closed his eyes and had almost drifted off when he heard an airplane in the distance.

Since Green River wasn't on any flight patterns, the only planes that came over were local, and Bud opened his eyes to see if he recognized it from his days as sheriff, when he hobnobbed more and knew some of the pilots.

He didn't recognize the plane as anyone he knew, and he lazily watched it, wondering why he hadn't gone flying since that fun time his buddy Tim had taken him up to look for the Slick Rock Cafe some time ago.

The plane had appeared over the ramparts of the Bookcliffs and looked to be heading for the Green River airport when it suddenly swung around in a big circle, then circled several more times, losing altitude with each turn.

Bud began to worry that it might be having problems, but the plane was soon back on course, heading straight for the little airport a few miles out of town.

A blue and green dragonfly flew by, and Bud wondered if any aeronautical engineer had ever studied its flight mechanics and tried to replicate them in an aircraft—though he suspected someone had. Maybe dragonflies and hummingbirds were the origins of helicopter engineering.

He then thought of the bumblebee, which had supposedly been declared mathematically incapable of flight by some engineer or other, and which, like a lot of theoretical calculations, didn't square with reality.

It seemed like lots of things lately didn't square with reality, foremost of which was the unreal image of Howie doing Shakespeare to rap music. The witches' cauldron chant drifted across his mind but was soon gone, for now Bud was fast asleep, his left foot twitching like he was one of the pack, following after Pierre and Hoppie, chasing rabbits through the Big Empty.

# 14

Bud woke and stretched, feeling as refreshed as he'd felt in a long time. Hoppie was digging a hole nearby while Pierre was watching, as if egging him on. Overhead, a raven was breaking off small pieces of branches, dropping them on Bud's head, which was what had awakened him.

He hadn't slept too long, maybe a half-hour, and the sun was now filtering through the big cottonwood at an oblique angle that spoke of dinnertime. It felt like everything was just right, and he sat there awhile, relishing the peace and quiet. He would get up soon and go home, hopefully just in time for a nice hot dinner.

It was then he remembered what Wilma Jean had said about having salads, and he wondered if he had time to run over to the Chow Down and grab a quick burger before going home for dinner. He could call it in and Karen would have it ready to go, though he'd risk driving by the Melon Rind and being seen by his wife.

Man, Bud thought, some guys sneak around to go play pool or have a beer, but he had to sneak around just to get a good hearty meal. Something was wrong with this picture.

He lifted the dogs into the FJ and headed home. Maybe he could sneak a bit of their pot roast and have a roast-beef sandwich before

Wilma Jean got off work. He then remembered the cream-cheese cupcakes and felt a little better.

Just then, his phone rang. He didn't even need to look at the caller ID, because he knew, as usual, it had to be Howie. Maybe there was some kind of filter on his phone or something, because it seemed like no one but Howie ever called him.

"Yell-ow," he answered.

But instead of Howie, a man with a low voice began talking. Bud looked at the caller ID, but it wasn't a number he recognized with its out-of-state prefix.

"Mr. Shumway, this is Julian. Lucy and Greg didn't make it to the rehearsal. I know something's wrong. He mentioned that Scottish play by name yesterday, and now he's missing. I called the hotel and cafe both, and they're not there. Frankly, I'm worried about them."

Bud was taken aback. He replied, "Missing? Did you call the sheriff?"

"I don't have his number. Your wife gave me yours. I figured you might have some idea of where everyone could be."

"I don't know, but I'll put out the word," Bud replied.

"Thanks," Julian replied, then hung up.

Bud stood, wondering what was going on, when his phone rang again. This time, it was Howie.

"Sheriff, we got a problem."

"What's that, Sheriff?" Bud wondered if Howie hadn't also just talked to Julian.

Howie paused, as if thinking, and Bud began singing an old Otis Redding tune under his breath:

Sittin' on the dock of the bay...

Howie finally continued, "Bud, I just got a call from Jim out at the airport. He said some pilot told him someone was shining a laser at him as he came over the Books. He circled, and it was coming from a yellow vehicle. You think we need to check it out?"

Bud was now giving Howie his full attention.

"Howie, are you at the rehearsal by any chance?"

"No, I had to go help some tourist look for his wallet. We looked for a good half-hour until he finally told me he thought he'd actually lost it in Salt Lake."

"Well, Julian called me a few minutes ago and said Greg didn't make it to the rehearsal."

"Maybe he was out looking for his wallet, too, Sheriff. That's the third person this week who's called me to report losing their wallet. One guy lost his up on the Swell and came down here to report it. You don't suppose there's some new guidebook out that's telling people to go to Green River to report missing wallets or something, do you?"

Bud groaned. "Howie, think about it. Greg may be missing. A pilot reports what might be a distress signal coming from a yellow vehicle like Greg's. Connect the dots, and what do you get?"

Howie thought for a minute, then said, "His wallet is missing, and he's missing with it?"

Bud replied, "Yes, and I think we need to get out there and take a look. Lucy's missing too, and I assume she's with him. We don't have that much time before dark. Can't be too optimistic with this kind of thing—we need to expect the worst."

"Roger, Sheriff," Howie answered excitedly. "Should I come pick you up?"

"That would be good. Better grab yourself some food and water, because we may be out awhile if we end up hiking."

"I have some cream-cheese cupcakes," Howie said.

"OK, bring those—we may need some extra energy. I need to take the dogs home and pick up a map, then I'll be ready." Bud didn't mention that he also intended to get his Ruger and its shoulder holster.

Howie replied, "Roger, Sheriff, and 10-4. See you in a few."

# 15

Bud could hear Howie's siren coming from town, and Hoppie started howling when it got closer. It must hurt his ears, Bud thought, wondering why Howie had turned it on.

He stepped out into the drive just as Howie pulled up, turning off the siren. Bud had a daypack with water, a GPS, a jacket, some maps, and a couple of roast beef sandwiches he'd made from the dog's crock-pot dinner.

He hopped into the Land Cruiser, and Howie backed out, spinning out while turning his siren back on.

"Howie, we really don't need that," Bud said.

"I don't want to run over anybody," Howie replied, then came to a screeching stop. "Where are we going, anyway?"

"Didn't they tell you where this vehicle was?"

"Not really. He just said it was at the foot of the Books. When Jim called me, the pilot guy was already gone, so he wasn't too sure."

"Howie, the Bookcliffs stretch for miles—all the way up to Price and all the way back into Colorado. They're probably 150 miles long, if not more."

Howie replied, "Well, it was somewhere around Green River, so that would narrow it down a bunch, don't you think?"

Bud thought for a moment, then said, "You know, I might have seen that plane come over. I saw a plane circling, and the timing would be right. I have a hunch it was the same guy—we don't get much air traffic. He was over by the Blue Castle."

"What's that?"

Bud knew Howie hadn't been in Green River all that long, so probably didn't know that's what it was called, even though it was somewhat of a landmark.

"It's a big castle made out of blue shale and sandstone."

"A real one? Out here?"

"Well, it's real, but it's not man-made, if that's what you mean. Turn right—it's out toward Gunnison Butte."

Howie pulled onto the main road and turned right, turning off his siren so he could hear Bud better.

Bud continued, "The Blue Castle is a weathered-out tower, sort of, but it has a big base, which makes it look kind of like a castle. It's all Blue Gate Shale, a member of the Mancos Formation, all marine, that's why it's blue gray. When you see gray shale, it's often marine, as the plant and marine-life are carboniferous and make it dark. It's pretty much at the bottom of the Bookcliffs and has lots of fossils in it, Howie, like that giant clamshell on display up at the museum in Price."

"How do you know all that?"

"I was up there with Wilma Jean the other day. She dropped me off at the museum while she went shopping. That clam's a good four-feet in diameter. Really something."

"How far do we go?"

"It's down the road a ways still. I'll let you know when we get close. It's just a two-track road that goes up into Blue Castle Canyon."

"So, that's what all those blue-colored slopes are over there, Blue Gate?" Howie asked.

"Yup."

The road wound through fields of alfalfa and melons, with a patch of corn here and there, big cottonwoods lining the irrigation ditches. The lofty Bookcliffs were straight ahead a few miles, where the road dead-ended at a ranch. A huge sweep of white Mancos desert pushed up against the fields on their left, and the Green River blocked the fields to their right, creating a wide swath of green in the middle.

Bud always loved driving up Long Street, even though out here, it was more of a road than a street. He enjoyed checking out all the other farms and the somewhat bucolic and rustic houses—most were well-kept, but dated.

"Say, Sheriff," Howie remarked, "You have something brown all over your shirt. By the way, did I tell you I talked to your friend Hum down in Radium?"

Bud was surprised. "You talked to Hum?"

"That's right, I personally talked to Sheriff Stocks. I asked him about the guy who owned the Silver Spur Cafe, and he said the guy had a long history of having a bad heart. I guess Hum knew him first-hand."

"Yeah, Hum knows about everybody in Radium County, that's for sure. He's been sheriff there a long time. So, I guess that means there wasn't any foul play at the Silver Spur Cafe?"

Howie grinned, "Hey, that rhymes. I wonder if I could turn that into a country-swing song. Let's see...hows about this."

> I took my gal out for dinner,
> And for once I offered to pay.
> But the cook came out and charmed her,
> And he took my gal away,
> Foul play at the Silver Spur Cafe,
> Yeah, foul play, yeah, yeah.

Bud grinned. "Hey, that's great, Howie. OK, turn here."

A faint two-track road cut off Long Street and headed west toward the ramparts of the Books, which were now a mere half-mile or so away. Howie turned, and they immediately were following a wash that appeared to go right under the cliffs of a huge castle-like butte of blue shale.

"That's the Blue Castle, huh?" Howie asked, pointing.

"Yeah, and that's where I saw the plane circling. Stop for a minute."

Howie stopped, and Bud got out, examining the road ahead. He was soon back in the Land Cruiser.

"There's been someone come this way, and not too long ago. Howie, I have a suspicion that yellow Jeep may be ahead."

"Have you been up this road before?" Howie asked. He figured Bud had, since it appeared he'd been everywhere a vehicle could go in Emery County, as well as lots of places vehicles can't go.

"I have," answered Bud. "We're going to come around a big curve up here, right under a big pour-over. If that yellow vehicle's anywhere, that's where it will be."

"How do you know that?"

"Because that's where the road ends. But Howie, get out and take some photos of these tracks before we drive over them."

"Are you suspecting foul play, Bud?" Howie asked.

"Who knows? But my years as sheriff taught me it's better to be safe than sorry when it come to potential evidence."

Howie took the photos, then they rounded a curve and came to a big pour-over, a place where the water was channeled off the huge rock cliffs and into the wash they'd been driving up. And, just as Bud had suspected, there sat a yellow four-door Jeep.

Bud jumped out, hand on the Ruger in its shoulder holster, and carefully went and looked in the window.

He instinctively held his hand up, as if telling Howie not to come over, but it was too late—Howie stood behind him, looking in.

"He never should have said the name of that play," Howie said grimly. "He knew it was bad luck."

# 16

"Sheriff," Howie asked. "Why is the Jeep turned around backwards? And look, all the tires are flat as a pancake. Do you think he was trying to get away and someone killed him?"

"He probably had just turned around to drive back out when he died, Howie," Bud replied.

"You know, Bud, sometimes I wish I'd become an astronomer. That's what I wanted to be when I was a kid growing up. Yup, today's one of those days I wish I'd gone to college and never heard the word *sheriff*."

"I understand, Howie," Bud replied solemnly. "This would be a good enough reason right here to change professions." He nodded toward the Jeep.

Howie continued, "Did you know you can see the Whirlpool Galaxy with a good pair of binoculars? It's 30 million light years away and 60,000 light years across. It's one of the brightest galaxies in the night sky, a classic spiral galaxy."

"I'm sorry, Howie. It just goes with the job," Bud said. He knew Howie was struggling, and talking about a different subject, about something he enjoyed, was his way of controlling himself.

"What now?" Howie asked.

Bud needed some time to assess the scene, and he knew he could do a better job without Howie around to distract him. Besides, he was kind of worried about him. Howie was sheriff and needed to learn how to cope with things like this, but he didn't need to learn it all at once, not today.

"Howie, you go back into town and see if you can get ahold of the coroner, Doc Austin, up in Price. See what he says—we can't do anything until he comes down here, but he may just want us to go ahead and have the EMTs take the body to the hospital in Price. But first, I'm going to stay here and do some assessment. We don't have long until dark. Get some photos of the Jeep's tires, just in case."

Howie looked perplexed, but took the photos, then turned to get back into the Land Cruiser. He initially looked relieved, like he was happy to leave, but now he seemed conflicted.

"Why did we take photos of the tires, Bud?" he asked.

"Just in case someone else was in here besides him, Howie. We can check the photos of the tracks against those of the tires."

Howie nodded, then said, "Sheriff, it's actually my job to look for clues. I need to learn how to do this, even though I might be running Howie's again by next week."

"Howie, you're not going to quit, you know that. But we're running out of time. We need to get this body out of here, and we also need to check out the scene really well. You go ahead and go back. I can fill you in on what I did for next time, OK?"

"Do you think he was murdered?"

"I don't know."

"If so, somebody must really hate Shakespeare," Howie said quietly.

He then looked at Bud for a moment and said, "OK, Bud. I know what you're doing, and I appreciate it. Thanks."

"Just don't strand me here like you did at the Silver Spur," Bud grinned.

"I won't," Howie replied, "Even though you weren't really stranded. I'll be back with the EMTs soon."

Howie drove off, and Bud immediately began to scope things out.

From the way Greg looked, he'd been hit on the head by something heavy.

Bud began methodically looking around the scene, now careful to not step on anything that could be evidence. The Jeep sat in the soft sand of the wash, the flat tires sunk deep, and though Bud examined them closely, he didn't see any slash marks or any indication of why they were flat. He also couldn't make out any tracks except his and Howie's.

He groaned, feeling like they'd violated one of the first tenets of investigation—not to destroy evidence by walking on top of it—but in their defense, Bud thought, they hadn't known they were dealing with a possible murder. He'd at least gotten photos of the tracks, which they'd now driven over.

Did Greg possibly commit suicide, killing himself somehow by a blow to his own head? That seemed pretty much impossible to Bud. Using a handkerchief, he carefully opened the door, gingerly examining the scene.

Greg's body was slumped over the steering wheel, and Bud carefully tried to figure out what could have killed him. It definitely looked like a blow, but there appeared to be no weapon nearby. Greg wasn't wearing his seatbelt, but nobody did out in this country, since the going was often so slow.

Could Greg have somehow hit his head on the window? No, a blow that hard would have cracked the window, and there was no blood on it. It was possible he had hit his head on the inside of the Jeep's frame, but Bud didn't see any blood anywhere.

He looked around in the Jeep as best he could and was satisfied he'd done his best when he suddenly saw something in Greg's hand. He carefully opened the dead man's fingers and removed it.

It was a bolo tie with an expensive piece of turquoise inset in the middle—and the tie was abraded and broken, as if Greg had ripped it from someone's neck. Bud wondered if that someone hadn't been the man in the Arizona car, for that was the last person he'd seen wearing that particular bolo tie. Bud carefully put it in a plastic baggie.

As he stood there, the sun finally went below the horizon, and the ramparts of the Books lit up in shades of magenta and red. Bud stopped and wondered how the world could be filled with such beauty and with death at the same time.

He now searched Greg's pockets, but found only the fifty-dollar bill he'd returned to him earlier. Bud was surprised to not find a laser pointer light, as that was what had caught the pilot's attention.

It was illegal to shine a laser light at a pilot, for such light could cause temporary flash blindness, similar to a camera flash, leaving after-images and blind spots. Laser lights could also cause permanent vision damage. If Greg had used the light, he'd hidden it before he was killed, but in Bud's mind, it was more likely someone else had signaled the pilot.

He could now hear a car coming, and for a moment he thought it must be Howie or the ambulance, but then his mind registered the fact that Howie hadn't been gone long enough.

He quickly ran and hid behind a big sandstone boulder that had rolled down long ago from the cliffs above. He carefully watched as a green pickup came up the wash, and he could tell it had oversized tires.

As the truck got close, whoever was driving slowed way down and almost stopped, then came to the end of the wash and parked.

Bud could make out someone getting out of the driver's side and walking toward the Jeep, and as they walked from shadow into the last rays of sunset, he could see their hair was the same purple as the clouds high above.

It was Penny.

# 17

Now, through the darkening shadows, Bud could see Penny tentatively walk over to the Jeep. She slowly and carefully looked in the window, paused for a moment, then turned and ran, jumped into the pickup and was gone.

Bud wondered what was going on. It seemed as if Penny hadn't known Greg was dead, but why had she come out here in the first place?

He stayed put, waiting for Howie and the coroner to show up. He hadn't really done much all day, but he was tired, and it felt good to just sit.

Leaning back against the big boulder, he watched as the night sky began to open, and he thought of Howie and his interest in astronomy. Howie had surprised him before with how much he knew about the universe, and it seemed kind of ironic to Bud, considering how little Howie seemed to be aware of certain everyday things.

But such was the way of genius, Bud mused—people who were super smart in some areas often didn't even notice things that others considered major.

Bud next began thinking of Greg, and he wished everyone would show up soon. He wasn't superstitious, but sitting out in the back-country with a dead man nearby wasn't really his idea of fun. Besides, his stomach was growling, and even a salad was starting to sound good.

He was watching a satellite silently move across the sky when he suddenly got a weird sensation that he wasn't alone. He sat very still, listening. It was obvious his intuition had picked up on something, and he was experienced enough to know that his senses were trying to tell him something, trying to make him pay attention.

Now he thought he could hear the sound of footsteps up on the rocks above him. He instinctively put his hand on his Ruger, removing it from its shoulder holster.

Cautiously peering from behind the boulder, he tried to stay hidden. There was definitely someone up there, for he could now make out a dark figure coming around the curvature of the Blue Castle above him.

As he tried to peer through the darkness, it occurred to him that if someone had been watching the scene of the crime, they would surely know he was hiding behind the boulder. Was the movement a decoy to get his attention while someone else snuck up behind him?

He scanned the dark steep slope that led up to the Blue Castle. Maybe he'd be better off moving to a new location. As soon as the thought crossed his mind, he began to feel panicked.

Quietly standing, he holstered his Ruger so he could use both arms for balance, then carefully began to climb across the steep shale, trying not to knock any rocks down and alert whoever was above him to his movement. He knew he would need to call upon his many years of experience out in this country, his knowledge of the different types of soils and where best to put his feet.

The flanks of the Blue Castle were made of bands of shale that had eroded into ledges, and he managed to step up onto one of these, following it a bit around as it curved. He then stepped up onto the next ledge and followed it around until he could no longer make out the vague shape of the Jeep below.

He was now a good 30 feet above where he'd been and wasn't feeling as panicky, as he knew he was now high above the figure he'd seen, but something told him to keep going, so he made his way around even farther. It was a tenuous business, as he could barely make out the ground.

Bud climbed higher and gradually felt his way until he was about 180 degrees from the Jeep, completely on the back side of the Blue Castle, when he finally began dropping back down to its base, finally coming down to the flat ground that surrounded it. He stepped into a stand of creosote, still feeling nervous.

Where was Howie? What was taking so long? He was starting to get worried.

He caught his breath. He wasn't in good enough shape to be climbing up and down steep slopes like this. But now the feeling of panic was back, and something was telling him to keep moving.

A sick feeling rose from the pit of his stomach, and he dropped and rolled at the same time he saw the subtle glint of metal in the starlight—and as he rolled, the sudden sound of gunfire was deafening. One, two, three, four, five shots were fired.

Bud rolled again and again until he rolled off the edge of a small wash, where he landed with a whump. He managed to pull out his Ruger and return fire, though he had no idea where to shoot, other than the general direction the gunshots had come from.

The shooter didn't return his fire, and for some reason, Bud got the impression they hadn't expected to be shot at in return, as if they hadn't expected Bud to have a gun.

It was then that he heard the sound of a siren coming and was silently thankful, for he could hear whoever it was now running away.

## 18

It was the next morning, and Bud and Howie stood under the Blue Castle, watching the big A-1 Desert Rescue wrecker spin out in the sand and then lunge forward a little, taking the yellow rental Jeep back to town on its flatbed, where it would sit in the wrecking company's fenced lot until Bud and Howie decided otherwise.

It was standard practice to impound the vehicle in cases like this until the sheriff was satisfied that no more evidence was forthcoming. Howie had contacted the Utah State Bureau of Investigation to come fingerprint it and do a complete forensic investigation.

Earlier, Bud and Howie had thoroughly searched the Jeep and found nothing except the keys, which were in the ignition. It appeared that Greg had been ready to leave when he was killed—or had possibly just arrived.

"Well, I'm glad to see that Jeep gone, Sheriff," Howie said. "It was becoming a public nuisance, always parked crazy. Say, look at all this blue shale here in the wash, right under where the Jeep was sitting."

"Did you tell anyone about Greg yet?" Bud asked, kicking at the shale with his toe, figuring it had blown down with the last big winds. He knew the news about Greg had to be all over town, with Wilma

Jean and Maureen both working in one of the two cafes where everyone came for their morning coffee.

"Just Maureen. It's not a secret is it, Bud?" Howie sounded worried.

"No, no secret. But don't tell anyone any details, Howie. I think we should walk around out here some more and make sure we haven't overlooked anything. I want to climb up to where I was hiding and see if there are any tracks from whoever was following me. Seeing how it's all shale, I suspect not, but I need to check out that wash back there, too."

"Maybe I should hang out and stand guard," Howie said seriously.

"That's probably not necessary," Bud replied. "I think whoever shot at me last night is probably long gone."

"Well, but what if they're not?" Howie asked. "They could be hiding right over there behind those rocks and we wouldn't know the difference."

"True," Bud replied. "I sure didn't suspect anyone was watching me last night until I found out otherwise. OK, you stay here and keep watch. I won't be long."

Bud scrambled up to the rock he'd hid behind the previous night, then made his way around the cliffs, trying to retrace his path. All he saw were a few places where the shale had been gouged out by his feet as he slid some, but no tracks that he could make out.

He finally came around to where he'd gone down into the creosote bushes then dropped and rolled. He could now make out a few broken branches and a place where he'd knocked off the rim of the wash as he rolled over its edge. Below that was a small depression in the sand where he'd landed, then his tracks as he walked back out.

He looked around more. Whoever had shot at him had also walked out, in fact, they'd actually ran, but he was having trouble finding any tracks. They'd stayed on the shale and out of the wash, probably intentionally.

Bud began searching the area, walking in circles that got bigger and bigger, spreading out. He was about to give up when he found one small depression in the dirt: it was a track with a squared toe and thick heel, like a cowboy boot.

He yelled for Howie, who was soon standing beside him.

"Howie, do you keep anything in the Land Cruiser for tracks? Like plaster of Paris or something?"

"I do, Sheriff," Howie replied, looking closely at the track. He then added, "The latest thing is this dental stuff. But isn't this one over here better? Maybe we should plaster it, instead." He pointed to a track so distinct you could make out the words "Made in America" on its sole.

Howie pulled a camera from his pocket and a small tape measure, and had soon taken a number of photos of the track. He and Bud then made a cast, which they wrapped in paper.

"I think," mused Bud, "That if we ever find the boots, they'll be easy to match to this."

"How so, Sheriff?" Howie asked.

"Look at this, Howie." Bud pointed to the track. "Three little stars up near the toe, and the rest of the sole has a distinct grid pattern. I would say this is a woman's boot."

"How do you know that? It looks like it could be either a man or woman, from the size."

"Well, men's boots usually aren't fancy on the bottom like that. And it may look larger because women's boots typically run a little larger than a woman's shoe, since you have to be able to pull them over the calf."

Bud now stood and walked away, then turned back and walked right by the track, leaving tracks of his own.

"Look here. See how much my boot depressed the dirt? I weigh 180 pounds, so whoever was wearing this boot weighed less—actually, quite a bit less. I would put them at about 120 to 130 pounds, based on the fact that there's about one-third less of a depression."

"So, we're looking for a woman who weighs about 130 pounds—a woman who wears cowboy boots and shoots a gun. Sounds like Annie Oakley. Did you look for casings, Bud?"

"I did, Howie, and I found these." He held up a small plastic bag with five bullet casings. "These will go to the lab, Howie, along with the track cast. But you know what's missing from the scene here?"

"What?"

"The laser pointer used to signal that plane. I searched the Jeep and the ground all around, as well as Greg's pockets. Nothing. If we could find and fingerprint it, it might be worth something."

"Bud, I never really thought about it before, but the one rehearsal I attended, well, Greg used a laser pointer for directing."

"How so?"

"He would use it to point to the part of the stage he wanted someone to stand on. That sort of thing."

"So, it was likely Greg was using the pointer to try to catch the attention of the pilot, illegal or not. He must have been desperate and unable to do anything else."

"Maybe he didn't know it was illegal," Howie answered.

"Maybe, but trying to signal someone who's in an airplane is the act of a desperate person, regardless, one who has no other recourse available."

Howie asked, "Bud, what do you think will happen to the Shakespeare production now?"

"I think they need a new director," Bud replied. "One who doesn't do rap, but maybe does country-western."

"Don't look at me," Howie said nervously. "I don't know the first thing about directing. Besides, I have a crime to solve."

"If we could get you in as director, Howie, it would put you in close contact with the actors and maybe help you solve the crime. And I have a feeling you'd do fine, especially since you're a musician and it appears to be a musical."

Bud was kind of kidding, and he had no idea how that would work, if at all.

"Maybe I'll volunteer for it, Sheriff, if it's in the line of duty."

"It just could be," replied Bud, as they got into the Land Cruiser and started back to town.

"Say, Bud," Howie said, tentatively.

"Yeah?"

"We adopted that cat. I named her Ophelia."

"That's cute, Howie. After a Shakespearean character."

"It is?"

"Yeah, I think it's from Hamlet. Isn't that where you got the name?"

"I just heard one of the actors talking about Ophelia and thought it was kind of pretty."

"That's cool, Howie."

Howie now slowed down, turning into Bud's drive.

He added, "Yeah, Sheriff, except Maureen says Ophelia's a male."

"Luck of the draw, Howie," Bud replied. "Maybe change the name."

Howie had now stopped in front of Bud's bungalow. "Oh man, Sheriff," he moaned. "How are we ever going to figure all this out?"

"I don't know, Howie."

"You'll help me?"

"I'll help you, to the best of my ability, anyway," Bud replied, getting out while thinking of Howie's earlier comment about Annie Oakley.

# 19

Bud sat slumped down in his big easy chair, mindful of the open window that looked out on the field behind their house, watching for movement and feeling uncertain. He considered getting up to close the curtain, but he enjoyed the pastoral view and hated the thought of sitting in a semi-dark room on such a beautiful day.

He needed to get back out to the farm and see what needed doing, but he was feeling out of sorts, which was to be expected, he thought, after nearly being shot the night before.

He rarely carried his Ruger after resigning as sheriff, but he was now considering carrying it all the time, even around the farm. He had no idea why someone would try to kill him—it felt like his world had turned 180 degrees around from the other day when he was napping under the cottonwoods.

He was seriously considering telling Howie he just couldn't help him out anymore, that he'd have to be the sheriff on his own from now on. After all, he'd quit his sheriff job because of stress and feeling like this, and it seemed like this was now even worse than when he'd been sheriff. He couldn't recall anyone actually trying to kill him back then, although a few had said they'd like to.

Bud now closed his eyes, and his mind wandered to the new Canon lens he'd just got in the mail the other day—a big 300 mm L lens, the kind the real photographers use. It was sitting on the table next to him where he could study and appreciate having it, as it would be the new centerpiece to his success as a photographer. He'd saved for it for months, and finally Wilma Jean had added enough that he could afford to get it.

The lens had cost more than his first car, an old pale-green 1957 Chevy Bel Air convertible with long tail fins and a Powerglide two-speed automatic transmission (low and high, and 0 to 60 in 12.9 seconds). Bud missed that old car and always regretted trading it in for a newer Ford pickup, as his dating prowess had seriously declined after that.

He held up the lens, looking through it at the dogs snoring at his feet, who were now suddenly tiny. Maybe he would become the Shakespeare festival photographer.

He'd recently won a grand champion ribbon at the art show up in Price with his photo of a big train fading into the sunset, even though he couldn't help but think it was a bit rigged when he'd found out the judge was a train fanatic and who also was friends with his Uncle Junior. He could've entered a photo of a coal car sitting on a siding somewhere and still won, he figured.

Bud set the lens back down and sighed. He'd pretty much lost interest in things since being shot at, and the truth of the matter was that he was afraid. It wouldn't be half as bad if he knew who was trying to kill him, and why. But to think someone was after you and not knowing who, or what kind of grudge they held, just made things hard.

But maybe he'd just stumbled into the wrong place at the wrong time, and nobody was really after him, he'd just been a convenient target at the time. Maybe they didn't even know who he was.

Nothing made much sense, he thought. Why had someone killed Greg? The guy wasn't even from here, and he hadn't been around long enough to make any real enemies. That meant it had to be someone from somewhere else who had known Greg before, and that pretty much narrowed it down to his acting troupe.

But why shoot at Bud? He hadn't done anything that would make someone want him dead—but maybe the someone who wanted him dead didn't realize that. Maybe they thought Bud had witnessed the murder. That was the only thing that made sense.

But why would they think Bud had seen anything when Greg was dead before he and Howie had arrived? And even if he'd just died moments before, whoever killed him had to know he and Howie weren't there to witness anything.

It was all very confusing. About all he knew was that someone had killed Greg and then tried to shoot him, assuming they were even the same person, someone who wore cowboy boots and wasn't very heavy, male or female.

He suspected the answers had something to do with the actors or the man from Arizona—and then there was the cook at the Silver Spur Cafe, who was still too sick to have any kind of visitors, according to Hum, who he'd called earlier, just wanting to talk.

Hum had been shocked that Bud had been someone's target and offered to send a deputy up to Green River to help, but Bud figured having a heavy law-enforcement presence would make things go underground even more and make the case even harder to solve.

Better that whoever had killed Greg didn't suspect that Bud was helping investigate. Bud would let Howie take over, and, as sheriff, that's what Howie was supposed to do, anyway. But Bud didn't like feeling afraid, and the more he thought about it, nobody had the right to threaten him.

As he sat there, his Scots-Irish blood started to boil, and he got up and started pacing the floor, fiddling with his pipe at the same time. Pierre woke up and grabbed onto his pant leg, dragging along, but Bud didn't even notice.

Bud wasn't a Buddhist, but he'd read a quote that he really liked from the Dalai Lama, and he was ready to implement it: "Change comes through action."

It was time for action. Bud picked up his phone and, for once, called Howie.

It was time to pay a visit to the Silver Spur Cafe and Desert Star Hotel.

---

## 20

Bud studied the menu, wondering how in the world coconut lentil soup had gotten on there. It must be a misprint, and it stood out among the standard diner fare like grilled cheese sandwiches, cheeseburgers, shakes, fries, and hot roast beef with mashed potatoes.

The waitress, Penny, came out of the kitchen and handed a bill to a customer sitting at the counter.

"Here's your eviction notice," she said.

She seemed to be in a bad mood, which didn't surprise Bud, given her discovery of Greg's body the other night.

"Very funny, Penny," the guy replied, leaving a ten-dollar bill on the counter. "Keep the change. And I like your purple hair."

"You wouldn't know purple if it bit you on the ass, Fred. This ain't purple, it's magenta. And that's about a fifty-cent tip, buckaroo," she answered. "Next time, you get to serve yourself."

"Oh don't get all wrapped around the axle," the guy replied, handing her a couple of dollars as he walked out the door. "I'll be back, and I'm gonna want more of that soup. That was the best thing this cafe's ever served—I can tell you that."

The screen door slammed behind him, and Penny came over to

where Bud and Howie sat, tapping her pen on her notepad, ready to take their order.

"You have bubble gum on your boot," Howie said, pointing to Penny's cowboy boot.

She held her foot up. "I don't see anything," she replied.

"Say, Penny, how's the cook doing?" Bud asked.

"Oh, he's doing great," she replied somewhat tersely. "He comes up with something new every day and is really turning this place into a gourmet eatery. Before long, none of the regulars will stop in 'cause the place will be full of Californians and uppity people from Park City. He's fixing Tuscan chicken-apple-leek soup tomorrow."

"He's back at work already?" Howie asked incredulously. "I thought he was in the hospital."

"Oh, *that* cook," Penny replied. "You mean Jackson. Say, aren't you the guy who helped out when we took him to the hospital?"

"I am," Howie said.

"And you're a sheriff?"

"I am."

"Sheriff of what?"

Howie pointed to the patch on his shirt. "Emery County."

"Never heard of it. Well, Jackson's still in the hospital, but he's not doing so well. He's not in any shape to come back to work."

"Who's the new cook?" Bud asked.

Penny turned to him and said, "He's some guy from Arizona named Bill. He just happened to be staying at the Desert Star, and when I put up the 'Cook Wanted' sign, he came in and applied. Nobody else applied, so I gave him the job."

"That's the same guy who made the cheeseburger I was telling you about, Howie," Bud said.

"Aren't you the guy who shut down the cafe for me?" Penny asked Bud, then continued. "Much appreciated."

"It's OK. What exactly happened to Jackson, anyway?"

"They say he had a heart attack. I don't actually believe it, because I was there, and he acted like he was choking and holding his throat. I tried to give him the Heimlich, but he just fell to the floor, and he's too big for me to get back up by myself. I think he ate something and choked on it, then had the heart attack on the way down to the hospital, or maybe after he'd got there."

"Does he have a bad heart?" Howie asked.

"He didn't until he got into the hospital," she answered. "I've read articles that say you should stay out of there, they'll kill you, what with staph infections and all that these days."

"You're right, and I bet a lot of people never get out of there alive," Howie added. "Probably a lot higher statistic than say those who go to a restaurant or a ballgame or something."

"True. What can I get you boys?" Penny asked.

"I'd like to try some of that coconut soup," Bud said. "Can I get a roll and butter with it?"

"No." Penny replied. "I mean, it comes with this thing called a ciabatta roll. Something made by the new cook. It's spelled with an 'i,' but you say it real fast, like 'chabatta.' He says he's into artisan breads, whatever that is, and is going to start making them. Tomorrow he's making baguettes, which he says is just a long loaf of French bread."

"French and Italian," Howie nodded his head knowingly. "They're worse than English for having secret vowels you never pronounce. It's like that muddled English that Shakespeare used, just confuses everybody. But I better stick with something I know, like a burger and fries."

Penny looked carefully at Howie. "Shakespeare? Like that production over in Green River? The one with the New York director?"

Bud was suddenly on full alert. He knew she was aware Greg was dead, as he'd been there when she'd driven up and discovered him first-hand out at the Blue Castle. He watched her closely, but she gave no indication that she knew Bud had also been there.

Howie replied, "Like the ex-director, you mean."

Penny seemed surprised. "Was he fired or something?"

"No, he died."

Penny now looked shocked. "Died? What happened?"

Bud now kicked Howie lightly on the shins under the table. Howie jumped, then looked at Bud and asked, "Why'd you do that?"

Bud tried to act nonchalant. "Sorry, was just twitching a bit. I do that when I need a smoke." He pulled the pipe from his shirt.

"Can I get a cup of coffee, too? With cream?" Bud asked, trying to change the subject.

Penny looked confused, started for the kitchen, then turned and said, "No smoking in here." She disappeared behind the kitchen door.

Bud leaned over and quietly said, "Howie, you can't tell anybody about Greg, other than that he's dead. You might tip someone off and give them information that we could use to incriminate them."

Howie replied, "You mean, I tell them he was shot, but they're the only ones who would know that because they shot him, so now we can't use that against them if they say they know he was shot?"

"Exactly. Best not to talk about it at all."

"Got it."

Penny came back out with Bud's coffee.

"Was this director guy in an accident or something?" she asked.

Howie pointed out the window and said, "Hey, Bud, look! There goes the Schwann's guy. His next stop is Green River. Maureen always orders these really good ice cream bars from him. She usually gets passion peach, but they have watermelon, too. Wilma Jean ever get stuff from them?"

"She does, Howie. That's where we sometimes get our vanilla-bean ice cream. Sometimes, during the holidays, she gets these things called frosted ice-cream trees. They have red and green sprinkles all over them. Ever tried them?"

Penny looked frustrated, then turned and went back into the kitchen.

"Good decoy," Bud whispered, grinning at Howie. "Nice job."

Howie replied, "Yeah, and did you notice how I cleverly got her to show me the bottom of her boot by saying there was gum on it?"

"Very creative. Did it have little stars on it?"

"No, but Bud, I wouldn't put her an ounce over 130 pounds. She probably has another pair of boots somewhere."

He then quietly added, "Bud, I have a question for you, something that's been bothering me."

"Shoot away, Sheriff."

"If it's bad luck to say the name of that Scottish play, why'd Shake-speare give it a name in the first place?"

## 21

"Howie, next time, try the soup," Bud was saying as they walked out to the Land Cruiser. "It was really good. I don't know where this guy learned to cook, but he's sure wasting his talents out here in the middle of nowhere."

Bud had picked up a few toothpicks from a holder by the cash register and was chewing on one, thinking maybe it was something that could replace the pipe.

As they got into the vehicle, the door to the cafe opened and the new cook came out. He was wearing a white apron over his shirt and jeans, but still had on the big silver and turquoise ring. He came over to Howie's window and kind of leaned in.

"Howdy, boys, you the sheriff?" He nodded to Howie.

"I am," Howie replied.

"I need to report a theft. I'm staying over at the hotel, and I came back the other day and someone had come into my room."

"They broke in?" Howie asked.

"Well, I'm not sure. I know I locked the door, because I'm careful that way, coming from more of a dog-eat-dog city environment. But there wasn't any sign of them breaking in, which makes me wonder if it wasn't someone with a key."

"What did they steal?" Bud asked.

"Well, it's kind of funny. I have some nice jewelry with me, especially a watch with a gold nugget band, and they didn't touch any of that. They went for my bolo tie—silver and turquoise—matches my ring here. My dearly departed wife gave them to me, so there's maybe more sentimental value than monetary."

Bud secretly poked Howie in the elbow as a signal to not mention the bolo tie that he'd sent in to the lab for analysis.

"That's all they took?" Howie asked, furrowing his brow. "Maybe you just misplaced it."

The man leaned back, shading his eyes from the sun. "No, I'm pretty careful about my stuff. I put it on the dresser right by the bed, as usual, and it was gone. It was stolen."

"Do you want to file a formal report? Like for insurance purposes?" Bud asked.

He was now feeling very wary, just like he'd felt when sitting in his living room looking out the window earlier that morning—like maybe things were no longer as they appeared, and not in a good way.

"No, it's not insured," the man answered. "I just want you to know to be on the lookout for it. Like I said, it has sentimental value. By the way, I'm Bill Birdsong, and I'm the new cook. I noticed you ordered the soup. Did you enjoy it?" He looked at Bud.

Bud replied, "It was truly in the top two bowls of soup I've ever had in my entire life. I'd say number one, but my wife would kill me, as she cooks, too. Where did you learn to cook like that?"

Bill smiled. "Le Cordon Bleu."

Howie whistled. "Isn't that in France?"

"Actually, it is, but they also have campuses in London, Tokyo, and Ottawa. I studied in Canada. I trained to be a pâtissier, or pastry chef, then I later added potager chef as another specialty, which means soups. They also offer wine and restaurant management and stuff like that. I later became a chef de cuisine, which means head chef. "

"And you did all this while on break from prospecting?" Howie replied, then added, "Just kidding. I thought you were from the Superstitions when I saw your plates."

"Not too far. I'm from Scottsdale."

"But you're working here now?" Bud asked, trying not to pry too much.

"Just for a short time," Bill answered. Bud felt he was hesitant to reveal too much.

Howie asked, "You ever been up in the Superstitions? Is it really all spooky and everything up there, ghosts of dead miners, that kind of thing? Man, I've always wanted to go up there, but to be honest, I'm kind of half scared to."

Bill replied, "Most of that's just talk, but there is one thing you need to look out for."

"What's that?"

"Dutchies, Dutch hunters. People who are obsessed by the lore and think they can find the Lost Dutchman Mine. Some of them have lived out there for years, and their brains are fried. They'll kill you if you go into what they consider their territory. There are over 100 people that have been brought out of there in body bags, and who knows how many more are still missing."

"That's pretty grim," Howie replied somberly.

"Yeah, and I heard that somebody around here was just killed. The guy who's been staying in the hotel. I've seen him around. What happened?"

Howie gave Bud a look, then said, "We really don't know."

"Wasn't he killed around here someplace?"

"He was, but I really can't talk about it," Howie replied.

"Well, he was an ass, if I don't say so myself. I saw him in action a few times in the hotel lobby. I don't mean to be callous, but I'm not surprised he had an enemy or two. But I need to get back to work. Nice talking to you. Here's my number if you find that bolo tie."

Bill handed Howie a piece of paper with his number on it, then Bud and Howie watched as he walked back into the cafe.

Howie asked, "You don't think he killed Greg, do you, Bud?"

"Why would I think that, Howie?"

"Well, he sure didn't seem to like him much."

"If everyone killed everyone they didn't like, there wouldn't be many of us left, I don't think," Bud replied.

"Well, while he was talking, I was thinking about my *WWBD* bracelet, and you know, he does seem suspicious, just like I've been thinking all along. And I was thinking, you know, what would Bud do? Bud would be checking out all the clues, so that's what I did. He's a small guy, Sheriff, couldn't weigh more than 140, and he wears square-toed cowboy boots."

"He does? I couldn't tell from over here."

"He does, and I think all this stuff about studying at Cordon Bleu was made up as a decoy. I bet he has something to do with all this."

"Maybe, Howie, maybe. But he learned to make good soup somewhere. We need to go on over to the hotel."

"I called them yesterday morning and asked them to not allow anyone into Greg's room."

"You did?" Bud was surprised.

"*WWBD*." Howie grinned. "Since that's where Greg was staying, we need to look at his room and talk to everyone. But I think all the actors are in Green River at the rehearsal."

"They're going ahead with the play? I asked Wilma Jean last night, but she didn't know," Bud replied.

"Yeah, the show must go on."

"Did you tell them you're interested in directing?"

"No. I just don't think I could direct anything, Sheriff. I have a hard time even directing traffic. Remember that time when the house movers had the bridge blocked and I had to steer people away? Man..."

"Well, OK, let's see how it plays out," said Bud.

"Good pun. Speaking of puns, did I tell you we renamed Ophelia?"

"No."

"We're calling him Tobie. You know, to be or not to be—Tobie."

Bud groaned as Howie backed from the parking lot of the cafe and headed the thirty or so feet to the parking lot of the Desert Star Hotel.

## 22

Bud and Howie stood at the front desk of the Desert Star Hotel, ringing a small brass bell that sat next to a "ring bell for service" sign. There was no one in the lobby of the old vintage three-story hotel, and the sitting area was strewn with magazines that seemed strangely out of place, not just with the hotel, but with the little town of Thompson Springs itself—*Shop Smart*, *Vogue*, *The Economist*, *Coastal Living*, and *Food and Wine*, the latter which Bud suspected was from the personal library of chef Bill Birdsong.

The others were probably from the free box down at the Radium library, except for the issue of *The Personal Lives of Gold Metal Olympiads*, and Bud had no idea where that had come from.

The hotel was clean and well-kept, but even what looked like new lace curtains over the tall windows couldn't disguise its age, and Bud thought he could smell a faint hint of old wood and underlying decrepitude.

Underfoot was an ancient rug that spoke of better times when well-heeled railroad travelers made money no object—thick and luxurious with an oriental pattern, though frayed at the edges.

Finally, an older gray-haired woman with her hair tied back with a paisley biker's do-rag came from the back and offered to help them.

She was small and wiry and acted like they were imposing on her, but she showed Bud and Howie up the stairs into what had been Greg's room, leaving them there to their own devices, assuring them that no one had been in the room since Greg had left.

Bud and Howie entered the room, which was neat and tidy, with the bed made up and a few clothes in the closet, along with a suitcase containing a pair of black dress shoes and the suit Greg had been wearing when they all got off the train.

The dresser drawers were empty, except for a hardbound book with the words "Holy Bible" embossed in gold on the cover, with the words beneath, "Placed by the Gideons." Next to that, as if competing for souls, was another similarly-bound book that said, "Book of Mormon."

Howie was now searching around the bed and found a brochure on the nightstand, which he handed to Bud.

On the cover was a photo of the Desert Star Hotel, obviously manipulated to make it look newer and nicer, with the words, *Utah's Fabulous Desert Star Holdings: The Right Place, The Right Time.*

Bud opened the brochure:

*Investors! Do you wish you'd been around to buy property near the national parks before they got famous? You know it! You'd be rich right now. Well, here's a once-in-a-lifetime chance to replicate that success, and this chance won't come around again, we can guarantee it!*

This seemed familiar, and as Bud read on, he realized it was the exact same text he'd read in the ad on the Internet. Just then, a receipt fell out and fluttered to the floor.

Howie picked it up, studied it, and whistled.

"Wow, Sheriff, this Greg guy must have had some money. Look at this."

He handed Bud the receipt, who studied it in equal surprise.

It read:

*Mr. Greg Anderson of 4069 New York 14, Geneva, New York, 14456, has paid Desert Star Holdings, Inc., Thompson Springs, Utah, 84540, a sum of $40,000 for four holding shares, with a maximum number of shares to be sold equaling 40, for a total of $400,000, at which point the investment offer will close and construction begin on the fabulous tourist mecca to be known as the Desert Star.*

It was signed by Zack Watson, Solicitor, Desert Star Holdings, Inc.

Now it was Bud's turn to whistle. "That's a pretty good chunk of change, Howie."

Howie asked, "What exactly is a solicitor?"

"Well," Bud replied, "It can be a lawyer, or it can just be someone trying to sell you something. No idea in this case which. Maybe even both."

"Where's Geneva, New York?"

"I'm not sure, but I think it's somewhere in the Finger Lakes region. I think that's where Yellowstone Kelly was from."

"How do you know that, Bud?" Howie looked incredulous.

"My brain's packed full of useless trivia, Howie. I remember seeing the movie a long time ago. They showed his mom back in Geneva, New York, when he was asking for permission to join the army. Yellowstone Kelly went West and became a famous trapper and saved a Sioux chief. They made the movie in the late 1950s, and when I saw it, I was a pretty impressionable lad. I wanted to go West and become a trapper."

"Well, did you?"

"Well, yeah, the going West part was easy, since I already lived there, but I never could get interested in the trapping and fighting Indians part, especially since none of the Sioux lived very close to Green River, and I like animals too much to want to trap them."

Howie replied, "Yeah, and hey, you should see Tobie chasing after Bodie. They're really a cute pair."

"Who's Bodie?" Bud asked.

"Tobie's litter mate. Maureen found out where Tobie came from. He belonged to this old woman who died a few weeks ago, and she had another cat, too, so we took it. Her daughter had been looking for homes for them."

"Wow, that's really nice of you guys."

Howie smiled, then suddenly looked irritated. "Bud, this Greg guy's a fake."

"Oh? How so?"

"He led everyone on to think he was some big New York director."

"Well, Howie, he was from New York. What's the deception?"

"The Finger Lakes is not the same as New York City."

"I don't recall him ever saying he was from New York City, Howie, just New York. But let's finish up here."

They were about done when Bud asked, "Did you go through the closet?"

Howie replied, "Nothing unusual there, Sheriff. But look what I just found in the nightstand drawer, right next to the phone book."

Howie carefully held up a laser-light pointer.

"That's impossible," Bud said in surprise.

Howie replied, "Double, double, toil and trouble, Sheriff. Hand me one of those plastic baggies from your pocket."

## 23

"He probably had more than one pointer," Howie said, steering the Land Cruiser onto the freeway.

"I'm sure that he did, Howie," Bud said. "I was just thinking that was the original one, but I obviously wasn't thinking straight. You just don't see laser pointers around Green River very often—ultraviolet pointers, yes, but laser ones, no."

"Why would you see ultraviolet ones, Bud? I've never seen one."

"Scorpion hunting at night," Bud replied. "Sometimes the kids do it."

"Why ultraviolet?"

"The scorpions glow a bright blue in the violet light. They really stand out and are actually very pretty."

"A scorpion? Pretty?" Howie asked.

"Well, OK, the *color* is pretty. Anyway, you can get them at the grocery store in the camping section."

"I think I'm going to get one, Sheriff. Are they expensive?"

"Nah, less than ten bucks. Just don't point them at anyone's eyes. But what you might seriously consider getting is a PLB. I was going to order a couple before I quit as sheriff, but never did," Bud replied.

"What's a PLB?"

"A personal locator beacon. It's about the size of a small cell phone and you set it off when you have no cell signal and need emergency rescue. It sends a signal to satellites, which then goes into the search and rescue network, and they contact the guys nearest you. They're only a few hundred dollars. Lots of sheriff's officers now carry them, and lots of outdoors people, too."

"If Greg had one, he would've been rescued sooner?"

"Maybe."

"Bud..." Howie said distractedly.

"Yeah?"

As Howie drove along, Bud watched a freight train on the tracks paralleling the freeway, though about a half-mile distant. He began counting the cars, patiently waiting for Howie to continue. When he got to 27, Howie finally asked, "Who do you think killed Greg?"

"I don't know, Howie. I really don't. We need a motive, and other than Greg being a difficult person, I don't have one. People aren't usually killed for being difficult, though sometimes you'd like to."

"Do you think it has anything to do with the hotel money? I mean, the guy running the hotel obviously scammed Greg out of a lot of money."

Bud replied thoughtfully, "Well, I'm not sure scammed is the right word. You and I may be able to predict the outcome of a scheme like that, but maybe the hotel guy really thinks he can make something out of it. And why would he kill someone who was such a lucrative investor?"

Howie replied, "Maybe so he wouldn't have to pay him back."

"Well, maybe, but you would think that would happen after the whole thing had folded. I think it's too early in the game to be killing off investors. Might not be so good for convincing other people to invest, if you know what I mean."

Howie now took the freeway exit for Green River, then asked, "Do you think it was Lucy, or maybe Penny? If it was the same person that shot at you...and as far as that goes, that Bill the chef guy could fill those boots." Howie speculated.

"I have considered all of them, Howie, but again, what's the motive?"

"I'm thinking maybe Bill didn't really get his bolo tie stolen, but had it ripped from his neck while murdering Greg."

"It does appear to have been torn off," Bud replied. "I'm hoping the lab will have something on that."

"What could they find?" Howie asked, now pulling up to the sheriff's office.

"Well, Howie, tiny pieces of abraded skin would be my guess. But there has to be some piece of the puzzle we don't have," Bud replied. "Anyway, here we are. You going to the rehearsal now?"

"I guess so," Howie answered. "What about you? You're already here in town, might as well come."

"Maybe next time," Bud said. "I need to go out and check on some things out at the farm. I've been neglecting my job."

With that, Bud got into his FJ and headed back toward home. He'd stop and take a break and let the dogs out, then get on out to the farm.

He was still feeling nervous at having been shot at, and was actually wanting to lay low for awhile, but he wasn't sure where. If someone were after him, it was pretty easy to figure out where to find him—home, at the farm, or running around with Howie, or at the Melon Rind or Chow Down. That was pretty much his circuit.

Bud stopped at the house to pick up the dogs. He noticed a plastic tub on the counter filled with what looked to be caramel cupcakes, so he grabbed a couple to take with him, wrapping them in a paper towel.

As he drove out Long Street toward Krider's, licking the butter cream frosting off a cupcake, he began wondering more and more about the bolo tie. He had a hunch, and he wanted to check it out.

He came to Krider's farm, and instead of turning down the lane, he kept going until he came to the little two-track that led up under Blue Castle and ended in the spot where Greg's body had been found.

Bud turned off the main road, then stopped there, looking around to make sure nobody was nearby, then let the dogs out. They were excited and started running around, sniffing and checking everything out.

Bud's hunch involved a tree or large bush, but there didn't appear to be any around to check out. He began climbing the blue shale to get a better vantage point, the dogs following, little Pierre slipping backwards one step for every two steps forward until Bud picked him up.

As Bud leaned over, that's when he saw it—there, down on the banks of the wash a ways below them, grew a small juniper tree right in the middle of a small stand of creosote bush, or greasewood, its seed obviously blown in from some tree far away, as the desert here was typically too dry even for junipers.

He sat Pierre back down, then skidded down the steep slope to the wash, the dogs at his heels. He was mindful of finding possible tracks, though by now the summer breeze would have made them less distinct.

Bud pushed through the greasewood and was soon next to the small tree. He didn't understand how the tree had survived, as greasewood was notorious for putting out a poison that eliminated its competition, but there the little juniper stood.

And now, his suspicion was confirmed. Whoever had been here before had also spied the tree, for they'd needed help in creating a decoy, and the tree had been the perfect assistant.

All along one side of the tree were abrasion marks, and Bud managed to also find a small threadlike piece of leather. Small pieces of bark lay on the ground.

He now knew he'd found where the bolo tie had been staged to look like it had been ripped from someone's neck, the tree used to saw the tie into two pieces.

It appeared that whoever had killed Greg Anderson was trying to frame someone else for the murder—and it looked like that someone else was Bill Birdsong.

# 24

Bud was back home, kicked back in his recliner, Pierre in his lap and Hoppie sleeping on the floor. He was reading a book Wilma Jean had brought home called "Directing for Fun and Profit."

She wanted Bud to read it and give her some idea of what the job entailed, as it looked like she might have to take over the play. He had decided to take a quick look at it before going back out to the farm.

So far, none of the Shakespeare actors had shown any interest in directing, as they all held the opinion that, seeing what had happened to the previous director, it might be bad luck to step into his shoes.

Bud was worried Wilma Jean might try to cajole him into taking over the job, but she'd already assured him he probably wouldn't have to, given his penchant for falling asleep in the few plays she'd taken him to in the past.

He took a sip of watermelon spritzer, careful not to spill it onto the library book, especially since it was an interlibrary loan book with the words, *Property of the Paradise, Utah Library* stamped in red on the inside cover. He wondered how many had left Paradise to pursue directing careers. He opened the book to the preface and began reading.

*Directing is a difficult profession that can take years to break into, as well as a lot of stamina and a serious talent for bossiness. In addition, directors have the stigma of being prima donnas, and some people find them difficult to deal with, especially if they're prima donnas themselves.*

*Good directors are hard to come by, and they've usually risen through the ranks of bad actors, giving them an insider's view of what a good director needs to do, having been on the receiving end of things. This gives them perspective.*

*A good director must love actors and be willing to put up with the many idiosyncrasies of these remarkable creatures. In addition, a good director frequently goes to the theater, mingling with the patrons afterwards, preferably over fine wines.*

Bud put the book down, figuring his days as a director were numbered at about zero, as he didn't fit any of those criteria. He wasn't much for wines (fine or not), he had never acted (even though he knew he would probably fit the criterion of being a bad actor), and, humble as he was, he didn't really think of himself as a prima donna (or any other kind of donna, for that matter).

Bud now started scratching Pierre's back, waking the little dog, whose right hind leg started compulsively moving at the same speed as Bud's scratching.

He then pulled the pipe from his pocket and started chewing on the stem. He'd forgotten to ask Wilma Jean to get a box of toothpicks at the store. He'd have to pick them up next time he was in town.

Just then, his phone rang.

He groaned, thinking it was probably Howie, but when he looked at the caller ID, he realized it was his wife. She probably had some errand or chore around the house she wanted him to do, and he was enjoying doing nothing, but he answered anyway.

"Yell-ow."

"Hon, you heard from Howie lately, like in the last few minutes or so?" she asked.

"No, is everything OK?"

"Well, I came out to sweep off the front step of the cafe, and I noticed a flashing red light down the street by the park. It looks like he's got a big bus pulled over."

"Like a Greyhound or something?"

"No, a school bus. All I can see is the tail end of it, but it looks like he's pulled over a big school bus. Why would he pull over a school bus? I hope it's not Mr. Jensen. He has health problems and really shouldn't even be driving."

"Well, why would there be a school bus out in the summer? Isn't school out?"

"Oh, I thought of that, but maybe it's someone on a field trip or some kind of school event. I thought you might know, since he calls you all the time."

"Well, he hasn't been calling me as much since he got that bracelet."

"I know. Maureen showed it to me before she gave it to him. But I gotta run, hon. Could you set the sprinkler on the apple tree before you go to work? See you tonight."

Bud had no sooner hung up the phone than Howie called.

"Yell-ow."

Howie was excited. "Sheriff, we got a problem. I tried my best to think this one through on my own, but I need your advice."

"Go ahead, Howie."

Bud patiently waited, thinking maybe he should research whether or not there was some reason why Howie always took so long to answer—maybe he'd find something on the Internet that would help him understand. In the meantime, he started humming an old Freddie Fender song, *Wasted Days and Wasted Nights*.

Finally, Howie asked, "You still there, Sheriff?"

"Still here."

"Well, there's this old school bus, and it's a really long one, must be thirty or forty feet long, and it's parked here by the park."

"Is that a problem, Howie?"

"Well, kind of, because it's parked kind of funny."

"Oh, how so?"

"Some of it's sticking out in the street. So anyway, I turned on my lights so nobody would run into it. It's a bunch of hippie kids, Bud, and you should see this bus. Man..."

"Well, sounds to me you have everything under control."

"Not really, Sheriff. I decided to run the plates on it, and they don't match. They're from a 1968 VW bus. So, I got out and talked to them—they're broke down—and right then, a 1968 VW bus pulls up."

"Kind of an interesting coincidence, if I don't say so."

"Yeah, and another bunch of hippie kids jump out of it, and they go and talk to the others, and now they're swapping off the plates, putting the VW plates on the bus and vice versa. I'm not sure what's going on, Sheriff, but it sure feels fishy to me."

"Well, maybe you should run the other rig's plates and see if they match an old school bus."

"I'm thinking that maybe they have friends who help them steal vehicles or something. I may need some backup, Sheriff."

"Howie, run the other plates and see what they belong to—it might just be a school bus."

"You think so?" Howie sounded relieved.

"I'm not sure, but I have a hunch they might. You know how these hippie kids can be, you know, live free, don't worry, that kind of thing. They don't tend to take the law as seriously as we do, Sheriff, but that doesn't mean they're necessarily breaking it intentionally."

"OK, I'll run the plates. But say, Sheriff, I need to go. Somebody's trying to call me, and the caller ID says it's the Air Force Coordination Rescue Center. Why would they be calling me?"

"Howie, I'm gonna go. You need to take that call. That's the national headquarters for search and rescue. Remember when we were talking about personal locator beacons? It means they've received a notification from a PLB that someone's in trouble. I'm hanging up now."

"10-4, Sheriff."

# 25

Bud poured water into the percolator coffee pot, then waited for the coffee to brew, all the time expecting a call from Howie.

It wasn't every day one got a call from the Air Force Coordination Rescue Center, and when one did, it usually triggered a search and rescue, or SAR, effort, which typically meant going out to some remote area, which included most of Emery County. The Air Force Coordination Rescue Center was the central receiving center for SAR requests beamed off satellites, and these always came from people with PLBs.

Bud wondered who had triggered the PLB and why. And he wondered if he would be needed to help, as he still served with the local SAR unit, such that it was, usually just him and a couple of EMTs, with the official unit being based in Radium, an hour's drive away.

He put a dollop of vanilla-bean ice cream into his coffee, then went outside and wandered around the yard a bit, the dogs following at his heels. He turned on the sprinkler under the apple tree, pulled a few weeds, uprighted the tipped-over wheelbarrow, then went back inside.

He was almost ready to call Howie, but instead fiddled with his pipe, deciding to go on out to the farm. If Howie needed him, he would call—nothing had ever stopped him from calling before, no matter how inopportune the time.

Bud checked out the cookie jar, which was empty, then looked in the fridge, where he struck paydirt—a container of what looked like malted-chocolate cupcakes. It looked like Wilma Jean was on a cupcake-making binge, which was fine by him.

Bud was guessing these were malted-chocolate cupcakes because of the color—they weren't as dark as real chocolate ones would be. The frosting was all swirled on like when one uses one of those frosting baggie things—he'd seen one the time Wilma Jean had dragged him into the gourmet cooking shop over in Grand Junction —and the cupcake had tiny white sugar stars sprinkled all over everything. It looked like something out of a fancy cupcake shop, and Bud almost felt guilty taking it.

He was beginning to feel like a foodie, a gourmand, given the gourmet cupcakes Wilma Jean had been bringing home lately, as well as the gourmet cheeseburger and soup he'd had at the Silver Spur Cafe. He was also beginning to wonder if he might just lose his taste for normal good cooking if this continued.

Maybe he should back off, he thought—but only after this one cupcake. He put it into a plastic sandwich bag and stuffed it into his shirt pocket. He knew he had just smashed it, but he also knew it would taste the same.

Bud now went outside, lifting Pierre and Hoppie into the FJ, then headed out for Krider's Melon Farm. Professor Krider was still down in Texas visiting family and wasn't scheduled to return for several weeks. There wasn't much to do on the farm, but Bud wanted to go check things out and make sure the weeds weren't taking over.

He also needed to check the PTO on one of the tractors, as it appeared to be leaking a little oil. He knew it was probably going to need a new seal and gasket, which he would have to order.

Bud was kind of looking forward to the job, as he enjoyed mechanicing, as long as it wasn't anything too serious. It was kind of a zen-like way to pass the time—kind of like a higher-level fiddling—a method for getting his mind off whatever was bothering him, which usually wasn't much, at least when people weren't shooting at him.

Once out at the farm, Bud walked the ditch bank around a couple of the fields, the dogs following and playing in the irrigation water. He was still feeling a little gun shy, wondering if whoever had tried to shoot him the other night was still interested or not. He hoped not.

It had now been a couple of hours, and still no call back from Howie. Bud sat down under that same big cottonwood he always sat under, pulled out his pipe, and began to fiddle and think.

He wondered how it was that things had transpired to the point where he felt like something was wrong if Howie didn't call him regularly. Hadn't he quit his job as sheriff to get away from that feeling of obligation, that feeling that something was always lingering just around the corner, that feeling of never being able to truly relax because of what might be coming down the pike—or in this case, Long Street?

It seemed like Howie had unwittingly put him in a position of being his ongoing advisor, which had been fine at the beginning when Howie was just getting started, but which was now feeling like an unpaid job. Not that Bud wanted any money, he was just wanting some peace and quiet.

Or did he? This *WWBD* bracelet had definitely resulted in fewer calls from Howie, but now Bud couldn't help himself, he was feeling out of the loop, like something was going on and he wasn't needed. What about the call Howie had received from the Air Force? What important things were going on while he was out here puttering around?

Bud pulled out the now-mashed cupcake—sure enough, malted chocolate. He slowly licked off the frosting, then ate the cake part, wadding the cupcake holder up and sticking it back into his shirt pocket, reminding himself to take it out before putting the shirt in the wash.

Bud wondered how in the world Howie was going to ever solve Greg's murder, especially when his time was always taken up by things like lost wallets and broken-down hippie buses.

He knew he should probably be helping Howie more, but Bud wasn't getting paid for this any more, and he sure didn't like the feeling of being a target, even though he was a moving one. But yet he had to admit he was a little bored right now, especially since things were slow on the farm.

He pulled out his cell phone and dialed the number for the Carbon County Coroner, who also acted as the coroner for Emery County, since it was such a small jurisdiction people-wise, if not land-wise.

A woman's voice answered, "Carbon County Court House, to whom should I direct your call?"

"Dr. Austin, please."

The call was transferred, and a man answered, "Doc Austin."

Doc Austin had been the assistant coroner before the previous coroner, Doc Richardson, had left, and Bud and Wilma Jean knew him and his wife Carrie well. The two couples typically ran the annual Green River Friendship Cruise together in the Austin's boat, going from Green River to Radium. They usually ran as the sweep boat, making sure none of the cruise attendees were left on the river.

"Hi, Doc," Bud said. "It's Bud down in Green River. How's everything going?"

"Hey, Bud, good to hear from you! Keeping your bow high and your transom above water line? How's Wilma Jean?"

"She's fine, Doc. You guys doing OK? We're going to have a nice melon harvest this year—better come on down. I'll set back the pick of the litter for you."

"Well, we need to get down and see you guys, since we didn't get to see you over Memorial Day because of the cancellation."

"Yeah, that was a bummer. Hope the river's up next year. Say, I'm helping Sheriff Howie out, and I'm wondering if you've finished your autopsy of Greg Anderson yet."

The doc answered, "You bet, Bud. Say, it's OK if I release this to you? I just finished it up."

"I was there, Doc. Was he killed by a blow to the head like it appeared?"

"Sadly enough, yes, severe trauma. But Bud, there was something else..."

Doc Austin paused, then added, "His cousin, which I guess is all the kin he has, she's made arrangements to have him cremated and his ashes sent back to New York. But Bud, even though he was killed by that blow, he was also shot in the chest, right smack through the heart, and it appeared to happen about a half-hour after he had already died. I find that really strange, don't you?"

Bud replied, "I do, Doc. Did you find the bullet?"

"Yes, and I already sent it to the lab."

Bud thought for awhile, then added, "Doc, it's strange only unless someone was trying to murder him and didn't realize he was already dead. I'll pass this on to Howie. Thanks, and I'll see you guys at the end of summer at Melon Days."

## 26

Bud's boredom was suddenly gone. Greg had indeed been murdered, or someone had tried to murder him, not knowing he was already dead. But who could it have been, and why?

Bud decided the PTO on the tractor could wait. He got the dogs into the car and took them home, then headed into town in his FJ, passing by the Melon Rind, then the park, where he saw a big International school bus, its rear end sticking out into the street, a couple of red cones set out to apparently warn people of the danger ahead.

Howie was nowhere to be seen, but a couple of hippie-looking kids were standing at the rear of the bus, as if trying to figure out what to do. Written in black paint on the end of the bus were the words, *Caution! I drive like you!*

Bud stopped. He leaned out the window and said, "Nice looking bus. Anything I can do to help out?"

He could now see that the entire bus was painted a bright metallic silver, and the front end sprouted a large set of what looked like moose antlers. The plates said it was from Colorado, but Bud wasn't sure if they were the correct plates, after Howie's report.

One of the kids, who was trying to dress like an old-time trapper, or so Bud thought, wearing leather pants and a fringed leather vest over a tie-died t-shirt, walked over to where Bud still sat in his FJ, window down. The kid was followed by another who kind of reminded Bud of what Yellowstone Kelly might look like after a few months in the wilds, with his long red hair knotted into dreadlocks.

"Nice of you to offer to help, dude," said the first, sticking his arm through the window and shaking Bud's hand. "I'm River, and this is Sage. We're thinking old Buckwheat is having a carb problem. The sheriff came by and left us these cones."

Bud got out of his FJ and looked the bus over.

"I'm Bud Shumway. I work on a melon farm here," he remarked. "Nice paint job."

"Thanks, dude. We're real proud of old Bucky. He does real good for a $500 skoolie. He's Buckwheat the Mutant Skoolie."

"What year is it?"

"He's a 1977 International Loadstar. 404 cubic inch engine, four-speed with a two-split differential manual tranny, and only 88,000 miles. Cool, huh? Even has AC. Terrible mileage, though."

"Pretty unique," Bud replied. "You boys overhaul it yourself?"

"We did," answered the other. "Except Starshine was the overseer. She's pretty good with mechanical things. She just went with Blaze and Raven to the parts store looking for a new carb. But dude, I bet we end up having to overhaul it ourselves, 'cause I bet the parts store doesn't have what we need. Wanna see inside?"

"You bet," answered Bud, ignoring Old Man Green's stare as he drove by in his old beater pickup. Bud stepped up into the bus after the two young guys.

"Dude, check this out," said Sage, his arms making a sweeping motion encompassing the inside of the bus. "Custom patinated bronze paint job. Did it myself."

The kid's smile was almost bigger than his head, Bud thought, wishing he was young like that again. He figured these kids had to be in their early-20s, at the most. They were out seeing the world, and that was something he certainly could approve of, having himself been bored just a few minutes ago and wishing he could go somewhere.

River took up the tour. "And dude, check out this wine barrel shower. See, you stand in the barrel, pull this shower curtain around you—that's a hula hoop rod—and this little water pump pushes the water through this hose and out this rain sprinkler. Gotta be careful not to run it too long, though, 'cause there's no drain yet. I'm working on that."

Bud whistled in appreciation, then said, "I like this hardwood floor."

"Starshine put that in. She even put it under the bed, where you can't see it," River answered. "And the ceiling is by Raven—unbleached muslin she got from a fabric store going out of business, and I put in the real mahogany walls from an old antique bar. Look at these antique brass screws I used. It's like a steam-punk gypsy wagon, don't you think, dude?"

Bud wasn't sure what that was, but he nodded his head in agreement. He then asked, "About that carb, does it put itself out when it's idling?" He was no mechanic, but he knew the basics.

Sage replied, "Yeah, it's running rich. Starshine knows all that, though. She tells us what to do and we do it. She's the boss and we're the minions. She's the scene-ster. We're a great team."

"Sounds like a lot of relationships I know," Bud grinned. "But where you kids headed, if you don't mind my asking?"

"Oh, we're going to the first annual Rainbow Man Festival," answered River.

Sage said to River, "Dude, I still don't get how it can be annual when it's just the first one."

"It's called optimism, man," replied River. "Optimism. You gotta look at the world the right way, dude, it reflects back on you. Like the plates thing, man. The sheriff was ready to give us a ticket and Raven and Blaze showed up just then, saved us from the Man, man."

"What happened?" Bud asked. He was enjoying hanging with the two guys, as they made him feel carefree and younger.

"Well, see, we accidentally had the plates switched with Blaze's

VW bus, dude, 'cause he's like that, a real airhead, but he sure can play the guitar—a real one, not an air guitar, though he plays that, too. But it all worked out OK because the Universe is an optimistic place, dude."

"So, what's a Rainbow Man Festival?" Bud asked.

Sage answered, "Dude, you gotta come to it. Being old is not a problem, not at all."

Bud was now feeling a little slighted and trying not to show it, but River added, "He doesn't mean it like that. He means that anyone of any age is welcome. See, we used to try out the Burning Man thing, but it was just too quirkster for our tastes. People were running around like, well, trying to outdo each other with their quirksterness, and we didn't like the ending where they burn everything up."

Now Sage took over. "Man, really bad stuff for carbon footprints, you know. We tried the Rainbow Gatherings, too, but they're kind of too much the opposite, they don't do anything but hang around and eat and talk about love. I mean, dude, that's fine, but it's boring..."

River interrupted, "So we decided to do our own thing. We're going to combine the best of both. Word's out, and we're expecting anywhere of a couple hundred people to show up, maybe even a thousand."

They stepped back out of the bus, and now Bud could see people starting to congregate over at the old flagstone square-dance stage in the center of the park. He'd forgotten all about the play rehearsal and wondered if Howie and Wilma Jean would show up.

"There's a play being rehearsed over there, guys, if you get bored," he pointed. "They need a director. But I need to run. Good luck on fixing this thing, and good luck on the festival. And thanks for the tour. You did a super nice job."

Bud got back into his FJ as the two guys stood there, looking like they were contemplating going over to check out the play. Starting the FJ, he asked, "So, where's this first annual festival being held?"

"Right here," answered Sage. "Well, not exactly here, but out on the edge of town. I hope you come, but be ready for a true scene-ster experience, dude. Tell the sheriff he's welcome, too. He said he plays guitar—he can come jam with us. He was real nice, would fit right in, a true individual kind of dude, an Alt A type."

Bud promised he would try, then said goodbye.

## 27

Bud could now see Wilma Jean's big pink Lincoln and Howie's Land Cruiser parked over on the other side of the park, and he thought of going to watch the rehearsal, but his fear of being conscripted as director overrode his interest. He drove on out the back street, hoping no one would notice.

He was soon on the old highway to Hanksville, heading toward the airport, just going to be going and with no idea where to in particular. The desert was wide open here, and he could see miles and miles of ridges and cliffs—Morrison Formation, dinosaur bone country—with the Henry Mountains far in the distance, deep blue triangles balanced on the distant horizon.

After taking a left off the old highway and driving a couple of miles down the road toward what he called Bone Hill, he stopped and got out, then began walking down a small wash, looking for petrified wood. It was his favorite thing to do, rock hounding, and it always put him in a zen-like state where nothing was more important than finding a cool rock.

It was warm, and after awhile he stopped to sit on a chunk of sandstone shaded by a bigger chunk, both tumbled down long-ago from the cliffs overhead. He leaned back and pulled out his pipe, thinking about the kids with the bus and wondering what an an "Alt A type" was. He'd have to ask Wilma Jean—she would probably know.

Checking to see if he had a good cell signal, he dialed the number of the Radium County Sheriff, his old friend, Hum Stocks.

"Sheriff Stocks speaking," came a gruff voice after the first ring.

Bud smiled. He needed to get down and see his old buddy—it had been too long.

"I'd like to report a UMO up in Green River," he said.

"What's a UMO?" Hum asked, curious but a little wary.

"An unidentified melon-like object," Bud laughed.

"Bud, you old rascal. You had me going there for a minute. You in town?"

"Wish I were, Hum, but I'm stuck up here in this bentonite clay. You know how this town is. Hard to find and once you've found it, hard to lose."

Hum laughed. "Well, you and Wilma Jean need to come down and go to Smitty's with me and Peggy Sue. No excuses."

"We will, we will," Bud replied. "Say, Hum, I need a favor. Is there any chance you go could down to the hospital and talk to that fellow named Jackson who cooks at the Silver Spur in Thompson? Any idea how he's doing?"

A small spotted lizard came out from the shade of a nearby rabbitbrush, then, seeing Bud, froze in place. Bud picked up a stick and scratched the dirt by its tail until it hid under a nearby rock.

Hum replied, "I don't think he's in good enough shape for me to interrogate him again, Bud, to be honest. He's not doing so well, last I heard."

"You already talked to him?"

"Yeah, Howie asked me to go in the other day and see what I could find out—said he was suspecting some foul play up there."

It appeared that Howie's *WWBD* bracelet was working, and for once, he was one step ahead of Bud. The tune to Howie's song, *Foul Play at the Silver Spur Cafe* popped into Bud's mind, though he wished it hadn't.

Bud asked, "What do you think, Hum? Did Jackson say anything that would lead you to think something's going on?"

"Well, I told Howie this already, but I do think there's a reason to be concerned, especially since that fellow was killed and you were shot at. I think it's all related. Have you seen anyone following you or anything like that?"

Bud looked around. He'd kind of forgotten about that. "No, all seems quiet. But Hum, why do you think it's related? What did Jackson tell you?"

"Bud, he could barely talk. I think he's going to be gone before long, as he's in bad shape. About the only thing he had of interest— and you know I trust you implicitly—well, Bud, I guess I can't tell you. I can only relay this information to other officers. If the right parties found out, I would lose my job without question."

"Does Howie know about whatever this piece of info is?"

"He does as of this morning when I talked to him."

Bud was quiet. There were only a few things that he could think of that Hum wouldn't be allowed to tell a non-officer. He sure didn't want to get Hum in trouble, which he could if someone were listening in on them, and who knew these days who was overhearing what?

"Hum, I don't want to overstep my bounds, but let me ask this— how long have you known whatever you now know?"

"I found it out just yesterday, Bud, after I talked to Jackson."

"Don't you mean when you talked to Jackson?"

"Well, Jackson alerted me to it, but I only found out who it was for sure after I called the Feds. You know, I understand the stress of being sheriff and why you quit, but sometimes I sure wish you hadn't. And to be honest with you, sometimes I think you still wish you were involved, the way you seem to keep helping Howie out. Maybe it's time to consider coming back. I have a position open any time you want it."

Bud paused for a moment, taken by surprise. Finally, he said, "Thanks, Hum. I doubt if Wilma Jean would want to leave Green River, given all she has invested here."

"Well, it's not that far to commute, only an hour, and the roads are usually good. I could give you four tens if you wanted. You could stay in our downstairs bedroom when you didn't feel like driving. You guys stayed there before, it's not bad."

"No, it's actually very nice, Hum. I could even get a little apartment and still come out ahead financially. Sometimes I really miss that redrock country. Let me think about it. I really don't think I could quit Krider after all he's done for me, but maybe I could work winters down there. Would that be possible?"

"Bud, you proved yourself beyond the shadow of a doubt when you were acting sheriff down here before, when I was in the hospital. Anything's possible, with a lawman of your caliber."

"Ex-lawman."

"I know, I know. Say, Bud, I know you're trying to help Howie, so here's something to chew on that might be a hint. Think of guys like the Mafioso, like Joseph Barboza. That's all I can tell you. And think outside the box—*way* outside the box. And good luck, my friend. I hope to hear from you about that offer soon. If you were my deputy I could tell you what I know, but at least Howie knows."

Bud replied, "Wasn't Barboza the famous Mob hitman back in the 1960s? OK, I know you can't say any more. Thanks Hum, I'll be in touch."

Hum paused for a long time, then said, "Bud, I may just get myself involved in this. Even though we have a joint jurisdiction agreement with Emery County, I'm not going to ignore something like this. Just so you know. Anyway, be careful."

"That might be a good thing, Hum. Roger."

# 28

Bud watched the little spotted lizard come back out to sun itself, then decided he should get busy doing something productive. He wanted to just forget everything and sit in the sun, too, but for some reason, he was beginning to feel an urgency, like he needed to get this case behind him, even though it wasn't his deal.

As he walked back to his FJ, he mulled over what Hum had told him, and it didn't set well in terms of his waning peace of mind.

Was there something going on in the little town of Thompson Springs that had to do with organized crime, with the Mafia? Why in hellsbells would anyone choose Thompson Springs for anything, except hiding out from—wait, was that what Hum had alluded to? Was Thompson harboring some kind of Mafioso fugitive?

He now leaned against the FJ and studied the puffy white clouds cruising overhead. It was mid-summer, and the melon harvest was just around the corner, and after that, autumn. After he wrapped everything up for the winter, he would have months of idle time to do whatever he wanted.

He'd spent last winter helping Wilma Jean around the cafe and bowling alley, as well as working some on his photography, but he had to admit he'd ended up looking forward to spring pretty bad before winter was even half over. Some of that was the cold weather, but some of it was boredom.

If he went down to Radium and helped Hum, he knew he wouldn't be bored, but would he miss having all that free time? On the other hand, their finances would be in a lot better shape. They were doing OK, but he could maybe afford another lens or two for his camera, things like that.

As he got into the FJ and headed back toward town, his thoughts drifted back to his conversation with Hum—why had he emphasized thinking outside of the box so much?

It certainly would be outside the box for anyone in Thompson to have anything to do with organized crime, Bud figured, but on the other hand, it would be a perfect place for someone who wanted to hide from something, whether it was a sordid past or even something as simple as wanting to start a new life, though Bud could think of better places for that.

As Bud turned right and merged back onto the old Hanksville highway, he began to again wonder about Howie getting a call from the Air Force. What had that been about? Did it also have something to do with this Mafioso person hiding out in Thompson Springs?

Bud suddenly felt like the odd man out. Howie and Hum shared some kind of secret that might help solve the case of Greg's murder, a secret he couldn't be privy to because he wasn't an officer, and this bothered him. He was used to being on top of things, and he was suddenly just a lowly melon farmer, which he hadn't minded one bit until now.

Maybe it was time to return to the profession he'd chosen when he'd first started with the sheriff's office a few years back—after all, his grandpa had been the sheriff of Carbon County for many years and never quit, he just retired when he got too stoved-up to do the job anymore.

But Bud knew that working in law enforcement was a burn-out position, and he'd been grateful to Krider for giving him a way out by asking him to manage his farm. Bud had no intention of forgetting all that.

As he approached town, crossing the railroad tracks, he decided he needed to just let Howie deal with everything. Hum could be his mentor, and there was nothing wrong with that, as Hum had always been a darn good sheriff.

Bud would go watch the play rehearsal and just relax, see if he could be of any help. After all, his wife had gone to a lot of trouble getting everything all set up from the beginning, this Shakespeare in the Sagebrush thing, and he owed it to her to be more supportive—except for directing, and he just didn't have it in him to be quite *that* supportive.

As he got to the park, he pulled over behind the old bus, Buckwheat, and got out. The kids were all gone, and he figured they were out looking for a new carburetor—probably had to drive all the way to Radium, would be his guess.

He sat there for a minute, Hum's words going though his mind —*think of guys like Barboza.*

Bud made a quick decision—he needed to see if he could figure out what Hum was getting at. And since the library was only a couple of blocks off, he could go do some quick research, then come back and watch what was left of the rehearsal.

He turned the FJ around and was soon at the door of the tiny building that housed the Green River City Library.

## 29

Bud was seated at the computer carousel, doing an Internet search on Mafia hitman Barboza, or more concisely, Joseph Barboza.

He soon found more information than he liked, as Barboza was a very unsavory criminal, and reading about him made Bud happy he lived in a little desert town out in the middle of the Big Empty. No organized crime here—there wasn't even anything worth stealing. But he was concerned that there maybe was organized crime nearby in the tiny town of Thompson Springs, as wild of an idea as that seemed.

But what exactly had Hum meant when he'd said to consider Barboza, and to think outside the box? Bud continued reading, and after looking at several web pages, he leaned back to think, pulling out his pipe.

Barbara, the librarian, quickly said, "Mr. Bud Shumway, what would possess you to think there's smoking in the library? What would Wilma Jean say?"

"That's a great rule," Bud replied. "I personally would hate it if anyone smoked in here."

He absent-mindedly left the pipe in his mouth and went back to reading about Barboza, unaware of the stern look Barbara was giving him. She and Wilma Jean were good friends, as Wilma Jean was on the Board of Directors.

Bud was oblivious to all but what he'd just read. Joseph Barboza was a Mafia hitman, alright, but he also had a soft spot for animals. Bud found this somewhat ironic, given the number of people Barboza had killed, but sometimes he'd felt the same way, preferring animals to people, though he would never kill anyone.

But what would that have to do with someone in Thompson Springs? Bud didn't even know if anyone there at the hotel or cafe had a pet dog or cat, so there was no way he could think outside the box on that one.

Now continuing reading, Bud discovered that Barboza was a skilled chef, graduating from cooking classes with a specialty in French cuisine, especially with wines.

This made Bud think of Bill Birdsong, the guy who had mysteriously showed up from nowhere—OK, Scottsdale, Arizona, so he claimed, anyway. Birdsong was a darn good chef, and he was exactly the same size as whoever had tried to shoot Bud that night out by the Blue Castle. Was he a mob hitman who was worried Bud had discovered his secret identity?

Bud continued his search. Barboza later turned FBI informant and entered the Federal Witness Protection Program, the WPP, where he was set up with his own restaurant, as well as promised plastic surgery, which he never went through with. He also enrolled in a culinary arts school.

The comparisons between Barboza and Birdsong were starting to reach critical mass, Bud thought, leaning back in his chair, though he hoped Birdsong hadn't killed as many people, as Barboza was rumored to have killed almost 30. But he had seen no signs of Bill having had plastic surgery, though how would one know?

Now Barbara was standing over Bud, arms crossed, tapping her foot. She sure acted different here than when she and Wilma Jean were sitting on the back porch of the bungalow drinking wine coolers, Bud thought.

He smiled, showed her the empty pipe bowl, then put the pipe into his shirt pocket, wondering how he was now supposed to think. Fortunately, he had a tooth pick still in his other pocket, so he pulled that out, then went back to his Internet search.

Bud didn't know a lot about the Federal Witness Protection Program, but he did know that it provided protection primarily to people whose lives were in danger from serving as a witness against serious criminals, and quite often these witnesses were criminals themselves.

They were given new names and IDs and sent into areas where the likelihood of being discovered was slim—places like Thompson Springs, Utah, Bud mused.

It was, of course, critical that the people in these communities not know about the hidden identities of their new citizens—except the Feds were required to notify law enforcement in the new community of the presence of the witness and their criminal history.

Bud sighed. Could this be what Hum had been steering him toward? Was there someone on the WPP living in Thompson Springs, someone who could potentially be a threat because of their past criminal history?

It made sense. Someone under the program had been relocated to Thompson Springs, and the Feds had told Hum's office about it, as required. Someone in Hum's office had forgotten to pass the information on to Hum, because Hum had just found out himself.

Bud stood to go, feeling like he was finally getting somewhere. Hum had told Howie as soon as he'd known because even though Thompson Springs was in Radium County and not Emery County, Howie was responsible for patrolling it through a joint agreement.

It was the same for the little town of Elgin, which was really just more of the town of Green River, though on the other side of the river. But since the river was the boundary between the two counties, Elgin technically was in Radium County. Howie was sheriff there also by a joint agreement, even though the two counties fought bitterly over who was entitled to the hotel taxes, since Elgin was where most of Green River's hotels were.

Now Bud sat back down, pulling out a torn piece of paper from his shirt pocket. He had almost forgotten to see if he could figure out if Greg's address in New York had any significance, the one he'd copied down from the receipt they'd found in Greg's hotel room.

He keyed in the address, and a website came up with a large photo of several people holding wine glasses up in a toast. That soon faded into one of a castle-like building with a large turret, then into yet another photo of a marble fireplace with a suit of armor nearby.

It was the website of a resort in Geneva, New York called Belham Castle, which appeared to specialize in weddings, fine dining, and tourist accommodations. He clicked on the fine dining photo, and up came more photos of a beautiful candle-lit dinner setting with a list of gourmet dishes and the credentials of their chefs, which were numerous and included graduates of Cordon Bleu, the school where Bill Birdsong had studied.

Bud got up and left the library, got in his FJ, and headed back to the park, parking once again behind Buckwheat. He was still chewing on the toothpick as he walked through the grass. He was having trouble thinking at all, it seemed, yet alone out of the box.

Had Greg lived or worked at the castle? Why would a third-rate theater director have an expensive address like that? Did he and Bill somehow know each other? New York and Ontario weren't that far apart, and Bill had said he'd studied cooking in Ontario. All trails seemed to lead to fine cooking.

But Bud suspected the hint Hum had given him had more to do with the Witness Protection Program. Greg and his acting troupe had said nothing about actually relocating to Thompson Springs and were only staying there to separate themselves from the rabble, according to Julian. It didn't seem like any of them were planning on being permanent residents there.

The only someone Bud knew that would maybe fit the criterion of actually moving there was the fellow from Arizona named Bill Birdsong. He seemed to be considering a permanent home there, given that he now had a job at the Silver Spur Cafe.

Perhaps Howie's suspicions were right, and Bill was somehow mixed up with Greg's murder. After all, Greg had held Bill's bolo tie in his hand, though Bud was pretty sure it had been placed there by someone else.

And why would Bill want to kill Greg? He admitted he didn't like him, but that wasn't a motive, and if he'd killed Greg, he probably wouldn't have admitted that he didn't like him, as it might be incriminating evidence.

Was Bill in the Witness Protection Program and had been recognized by Greg and therefore felt he had to kill him? And where did Penny fit into all this? Why had she come out to where Greg was killed, then acted shocked to see his body?

None of it really made much sense. Hum had said to think outside the box, but Bud was beginning to think he couldn't even figure out what kind of box they were working with in the first place.

Bud was puzzling over all this just in time to look up and see the devil himself walking toward him—Bill Birdsong.

# 30

"Howdy, Bud," said Bill, holding out his hand.

Bud shook his hand. "Hi, Bill. You been at the rehearsal?"

Bill smiled and said, "I watched a few minutes of it, and boy, is it, well, *different* might be one word. I was actually here to talk to your wife."

"Oh?"

"She wants me to start making some desserts for her little cafe. We're working out the details."

"I can say I approve of that," Bud replied. "Did she get the recipe for the malted chocolate cupcakes from you?"

"She did. But she's too busy, as I'm sure you know, to really dedicate the time necessary for fine culinary creations, so she's hired me to bake for the cafe. I'll be bringing stuff in three days a week for starters. We'll see how it goes."

Bud asked, "So, it sounds like you're sticking around for awhile?"

"Oh, I don't know," Bill said. "I'm just having fun right now. I'll leave when things get boring."

"Or maybe when things get too hot," Bud said.

"Does it get hotter than this? I was thinking this time of year was probably the peak for that."

"Guess it depends," Bud answered. "So, any leads on who might have taken your bolo tie?"

"I got it back, thankfully," said Bill. "Sheriff Howie returned it to me, said it was found out in the desert. I'm going to have to replace the tie part, but the stone is intact, and that's what matters."

This bit of news surprised Bud. He had left the tie in the safe at the sheriff's office. Why would Howie return it when it might prove to be evidence in a murder trial?

Bill now said, "My first creation for the Melon Rind is going to be what I call my Sweet Dreams Cake. It's layered chocolate and hazlenut sponge cake, topped with a rich Cabernet ganache and filled with a Cabernet poached pear mousse. I'm going to show Wilma Jean how to make it when the melons are ripe, using melons instead of pears."

"Isn't Cabernet a wine?" Bud asked, feeling a little outgunned.

"It is," Bill said, smiling generously. "The Sauvignon is elegant and very full-bodied. You have trouble getting good wines here in Utah, I would guess. I'll bring you a nice bottle next time I go down to Scottsdale."

"It's probably pretty expensive, I would think," Bud stumbled. "Unless one has a real good source of income..."

"Oh, I'll get you a bottle as a gift. Your wife is helping me, showing me the ropes around here. But I like to go to little towns and scope things out, though I'm used to being in a much more, well, shall we say, a more vital environment."

"Vital, as in a big city?" Bud asked. "Like ones with high crime rates and all that? Where people get killed?" He studied Bill's face.

"Oh, not every city is dangerous," Bill replied, his brows furrowed in puzzlement. "It's like going into the Superstitions—you just have to know who your friends are. Speaking of which, my gang's coming up soon and it's going to be pretty exciting. Well, nice running into you."

Bud said goodbye, feeling kind of foolish, yet wishing he could figure out what was going on. Bill seemed like a nice retired guy from the desert southwest, not some Mafioso, but you never knew.

Bud walked on over to the flagstone stage. It had been built years ago by some service group or another, and they'd done a good job, in his estimation. Red flagstone had been stacked and cemented together, building a large platform about four-feet high.

The stage had been used for a number of purposes by the good citizens of Green River through the years, including a place to square dance, as well as to hold concerts. It also served as the center stage for Melon Days.

Bud expected to see the play in full practice mode, but everyone was kind of just milling around, looking desultory. All the actors were there, as well as Howie and Maureen and the kids from Buckwheat the Mutant Skoolie, who were stretched out on the grass, watching, even though nothing much appeared to be going on.

"Howdy, Sheriff," Howie said, seeing Bud. "You here to direct?"

"Well, not that I'm aware of," Bud replied, "Though I've been known to do things I'm unaware of. Where's my wife?"

"She went to the cafe so Maureen could take time off to hang out with us. But we're not doing much 'cause nobody wants to do anything. We're stuck. I guess that's what happens to creative types, they get stuck." Howie said.

One of the skoolie kids now got up and walked over. It was Sage.

"You dudes want some free advice?" he asked.

"Sure," Howie said.

"Well, we've been sitting here watching, and the general consensus is, dudes, and peace out and all that, but we can't understand anything you're saying. See, we're not even sure which play you're trying to do, dudes, is it *Hamlet*? Or maybe *Annie Get Your Gun*? *Paint Your Wagon*? *Comedy of Errors*?"

He paused, and River took over. "See, you've got people standing around looking like it's a Western, like this sheriff dude here and this Annie Oakley dude here, and then you've got people acting all snobbish like they're doing something from Shakespeare, and it's not working, dudes. Like, we don't just use our heads to grow hair, dudes, we're a truly enlightened audience, and if we can't figure all this out, nobody can. It's like we're waiting for Godot and he ain't ever showing up, dudes."

Lucy and Julian were standing at the front of the actors, listening. Lucy looked horrified.

Now, a tall girl with thick blonde dreads stood up from where she'd been sitting by the other skoolies. She was barefoot and wearing yoga pants with a long white t-shirt with the words, *I am a missing person.*

Her eyes were framed by a big pair of black thick-rimmed glasses that looked like something Buddy Holly might wear, except there were no lenses in the frames. They kept sliding down onto her nose, and she kept pushing them back up, reminding Bud of his own sunglasses.

This had to be Starshine, Bud thought, wondering what the shirt meant.

She was excited, and addressing Sage and River, said, "Look, you quirksters, they're trying to do some kind of rap thing to Shakespeare. I agree it's not working, and that's 'cause rap is so totally overwhelmingly passé. I think they should do it to reggae, a kind of Bob Marley MacBeth."

The actors, who had been quietly talking among themselves, were now deathly silent. Bud watched as Lucy turned to Julian as if to say something—then, Annie Oakley outfit and all, passed out, heading for the flagstone deck until Julian managed to catch her at the last minute.

Howie looked at Starshine, dismayed, and said, "I think you maybe shouldn't have said the name of that Scottish play."

# 31

---

"What'd I do?" Starshine asked, confused.

Maureen was now standing by Lucy, who had recovered somewhat and was sitting on the edge of the flagstone stage.

Julian, after handing Lucy off to Maureen, had jumped off the stage and was standing next to Starshine, who looked puzzled.

"Look," he said. "You have to do what I say or we'll all be cursed. First, spin around three times as fast as you can."

He watched as Starshine did what he said, looking nervous and scared, her blonde dreads spinning around like kids hanging off a merry-go-round. River and Sage and the others stood by, also looking nervous.

"Now," Julian continued after she'd stopped, "Spit over your shoulder."

Starshine appeared to comply, though it seemed to Bud she hadn't put her heart into it.

"OK, now you have to say a line from the Merchant of Venice, a lucky play."

"But I don't know one," she pleaded.

"OK, repeat after me, 'He doth nothing but talk of his horse.'"

"What?"

"He doth nothing but talk of his horse."

"That's a Shakespeare quote?" Starshine appeared to be recovering from her shock.

"It's all I can remember," Julian replied. "It's when Portia is talking about the horseman who wants to be her suitor."

"OK," Starshine said. "He doth nothing but talk of his horse."

"One more time for luck."

"He doth nothing but talk of his horse."

"OK," Julian said, turning to Lucy. "Lucy, it's OK. The curse has been removed."

He then turned back to Starshine, who was now looking incredulous, and said, "Never say that name again around Shakespearean actors. It's really bad luck."

"What name, MacBeth?" Starshine said with an impish smile.

"Holy Shakes!" Julian muttered, going back up on the stage. "OK, time to regroup, people. We need to have an actor's confab. Everyone over to the Melon Rind."

With that, they all took off toward the cafe, Lucy trailing behind, walking with Maureen at her side, looking pale and shaken.

"You're an evil dude, dude," Sage said to Starshine, smiling.

"I try," she answered, unperturbed. "Anybody who's that superstitious deserves me."

Howie now went over to the bus and looked under its hood, talking to River, Raven, and Blaze about the carb problem.

Bud suddenly felt kind of wistful, trying to remember what it had been like to be young and carefree like these kids. He knew he'd been young, but he wasn't sure he'd ever been so carefree, as he'd married right out of high school and gone to work in the uranium mines.

He turned to Sage and asked, "What's it like to be young and carefree like you guys?"

Sage answered, "Well, we may be young, dude, but we're really not as carefree as we look. Star here's got to go back to school at the end of the summer, and I have to go home and look for a job or my mom's going to have a cow. And the other dudes, well, they all have similar stuff going on. Raven's got a boyfriend back home who wants to get married, and Blaze is heading back to work at the ski area—he does ski patrol."

Starshine added, "And River's probably the biggest slacker dude here—all he ever wants to do is set up his drumset out in the desert and play all day—and even he has to go back to his barrista job. We save up all year so we can drive this stupid bus around and break down in various towns. But dude, if you want to join us for awhile, you can see first hand what it's like. Come on out to the Rainbow Man Festival."

"I might just do that," Bud replied. "But say, I have another question for you. What exactly is an Alt A type?"

"An Alt A type?" repeated Starshine. "Where'd you hear that?"

"One of you guys said that about Howie over there, the sheriff. Said he was an Alt A type."

"You have a computer?" asked Sage.

"I do," answered Bud.

"Well, next time you're on it, dude, press Alt A and see what you get. That's an Alt A type."

Bud was confused. "I get something when I press Alt A?"

Starshine broke in. "Look, Sage is just confusing things. It's a cool band from Canada. That's their name, Alt A, for the silly little *a* with a circle on it you get when you press Alt A. That's all. If you're an Alt A type, it just means you're cool because they're cool. Like life, you have to create your own meaning with some things."

"Oh," Bud said, feeling a little confused. "Well, OK, and thanks."

"We're off to the races," said Sage, pointing to the bus, which was now sputtering and coughing between bouts of running smooth. "If they got that thing fixed, we're going to go find a spot for the festival. Any ideas?"

"Well," Bud replied, thinking. "I sure wouldn't go out Long Street. Too many things going on out that direction. I think I'd go out to the old missile base. Nobody will care if you're out there. It's land that belongs to the Army and they've pretty much abandoned it since they shot off missiles in the 60s and 70s. Just follow the signs that say

'Crystal Geyser' and keep going straight at the first intersection. Go on up to the top of the hill. Nice views, too."

"Cool. Thanks, dude," Sage said.

Blaze was now behind the skoolie's steering wheel, honking its horn, the others inside, as the old bus sputtered and wheezed and finally took off.

"Go, Buckie, go!" yelled Sage as he and Starshine ran alongside it, barely managing to jump in before it was gone.

# 32

Howie was now standing by Bud. He said, "Man, Sheriff, I'm sure glad they got that thing fixed, especially with it sticking out in the street like that."

He watched a cloud of blue smoke drift away, then continued. "Sheriff, we need some direction for this darn play. It's going nowhere, and we're running out of time. Are you sure you don't want to be the director?"

"Howie, I don't think I could do it, to be honest. But has anyone considered maybe doing a different play? Shakespeare wrote a lot more than that Scottish play, if I recall correctly."

"Well, there's a thought," Howie said thoughtfully. "They just did Romeo and Juliet, so I bet they still know the lines."

"Say, Howie, I was just talking to Bill Birdsong, and he said you gave him his bolo tie back. Does that mean the lab returned it with a report?"

"They did," Howie answered.

Bud waited patiently as Howie went and retrieved his red traffic cones, putting them in the back of the Land Cruiser, then came back over to Bud.

Howie then said, "It was just like you suspected, Sheriff. The tie had microscopic pieces of bark right where it was broken, like they'd rubbed it on a tree to split it."

"Were there any fingerprints?"

"Yes, and it's just like I thought, Sheriff. That Bill Birdsong is one suspicious character."

"Were they his fingerprints?"

"They were."

"And none of Greg's?"

"Nope. Just Bill's. I think he rubbed it on the tree to break it in two so it would look like Greg was struggling with someone, grabbed the tie around their neck, and held on until it broke. Kind of a sloppy setup, if you ask me. It would be almost impossible to break a piece of leather like that."

"But why would Bill want to incriminate himself if he killed Greg by leaving his own bolo tie?"

"I dunno, Bud. I think he was trying to frame himself so he'd look like he was innocent."

"How does that work?"

"See, if you're framed, everyone thinks you were set up by some-body, by the bad guy. So if you frame yourself, it distracts people from thinking it was you. You couldn't have possibly done it if you were framed, right?"

"Well, I guess not, by definition. But say, Howie, you decided it was the thing to do to give him back the tie rather than keeping it for possible evidence?"

"Well, I wasn't so sure, but I knew this Birdsong guy really wanted it back, as it was a momento of his deceased wife. Even bad guys can have feelings. So, I looked at my *WWBD* bracelet and decided to call Sheriff Hum. He said it would be OK, since I had photos and the lab report and there really wasn't anything incriminating there."

"Hum said that?"

"Yeah, and he told me..."

"What?"

"Bud, I can't tell you, 'cause he said not to."

"It's OK, Howie. I already talked to him, and he explained it all."

"He told you who was under the Witness Protection Program?"

Bud paused. It looked like his guess had been right, though he still didn't know who it was.

"No, he explained why he couldn't tell me. It's OK, Howie."

Howie looked relieved. He was now checking his watch.

"You know, I need to get back to the office," he said.

Bud walked over to the Land Cruiser with Howie. He had told Howie it was OK, but in reality, he was starting to feel that same outside-looking-in feeling he'd felt earlier when taking to Hum. He flashed again on the offer Hum had made, wondering if maybe he shouldn't seriously consider it. He'd have to talk to Wilma Jean.

Howie was in the Land Cruiser when Bud asked, "Say, remember that call you got when we were talking and had to hang up?"

"Which call was that, Bud?"

"You know, the one from the Air Force."

"Oh, yeah, that one, the Air Force Coordination Rescue Center. I remember."

Bud waited for Howie to continue. When he didn't, Bud finally asked, "What did they want, if you don't mind my asking. Was there a rescue or something?"

"Oh, it was some guy who said he was Captain Udink. He wanted to know how I was doing. I said fine, fine, and that was about all there was to it."

Howie was acting a little evasive, Bud thought, but wanting to know the rest of the story, he asked, "Why would he call you to ask how you're doing? Are you guys friends or something?"

"Well, we kind of are now. He said he'd stop in if he was ever in Green River."

Bud sighed. "Howie, they don't just call people out of the blue to chat. Why would he call you if there wasn't a rescue?"

"Well, Sheriff, remember when you said Greg would've maybe had help sooner if he'd had a PLB, a personal locator beacon? I talked to the mayor to requisition one, and he said he had one I could use. I guess the EMTs have them, and he had an extra. So I went over and got it, registered it, and decided to test it out. There were two little buttons, and one said *Activate* and the other said *Test*, so I figured you had to activate the darn thing before you could test it. Doesn't that seem logical to you?"

"It does, but that's not how it works. You push *Activate* when you're in trouble."

"So I found out."

"So, you turned the beacon on, a satellite picked up the signal, and they called you to see if you were OK because they had your number from when you registered it. I get it now. I'm sure you weren't the first one."

"He said I wasn't."

"Was he mad?"

"No, he just said, this is Air Force Captain Udink, your beacon is turned on, and are you OK? I said yes, and he said good, he was glad. He was a real nice fellow. Told me how to turn it off. See, you have to hold the button in for five seconds. Anyway, he may even be coming through here soon, he said, and I told him to stop and see our Shakespeare play, and he said he would. So if you see some guy in a navy-blue Air Force uniform, that's probably Captain Udink. He had just got a puppy, and I was telling him about Tobie and Bodie and we were just getting into a good conversation when he said he had to go, as he was getting an emergency call."

"Got it, Howie," Bud grinned. "And I'm glad you're OK, too. See you later."

# 33

Bud pulled into the Silver Spur Cafe parking lot just in time to see a big Utah Railway freight train roll by, a long coal train with two helper engines. The noise was deafening, as the tracks were right next to the parking lot. He wished he'd brought his camera, even though such trains were a daily occurrence in Green River, the next town down the tracks.

As he stood there, watching the big cars shake and rattle and listening to the clickity-clack of the rails, he noted Bill Birdsong's gray sedan nearby.

After the train was gone, Bud walked by the car on his way to the front door and couldn't help but take a closer look.

He'd assumed it was just another older gray-sedan type car, lots of those on the roads around here—but upon closer inspection, he realized this one was different—*way* different. It was a standard four-door sedan, but the grill and front-end with its long rectangular lights were fairly distinct looking, like something Bud should recognize but couldn't quite put his finger on.

As he walked around the car, he realized why he couldn't quite put his finger on it—it was a model of car he'd never seen before. He couldn't believe his eyes! On the hood of the car stood a silver robed figure with wings outstretched as if getting ready to take off, which Bud recognized as the famous "Flying Lady," or "Spirit of Ecstasy."

Beneath that was a square logo embedded in the grill with two big R's, one nearly under the other like a shadow. Above the two R's was the word, *Rolls*, and beneath that, the word, *Royce*.

Bud instinctively let out a long low whistle. He was looking at the likes that had probably never been in the lowly little town of Thompson Springs before, a genuine Rolls Royce automobile, the real deal.

He couldn't help but lean over to take a look inside. Sure enough, it had what looked to be real leather seats and a beautiful wood console, and the seats matched the silver exterior of the car, with a rich, deep carpet on the floor that was immaculately clean.

Bud was mesmerized. Even though he was more of an old 1952 Dodge pickup kind of guy, he knew a biblical car when he saw it. But it didn't take long for his instincts to kick in, those same instincts that had made him a top-notch sheriff.

Who in hellsbells could afford a car like this—except maybe someone with, as you might say, connections? You not only needed a pocketful of cash, but also to be able to locate one, which would take the right people, as they had to be rare. Not everyone had a Rolls Royce nor knew where to get one, as these were collectibles.

"She's a beaut, isn't she?" came a voice from behind.

Bud jumped, then turned to see Bill Birdsong.

"One of a kind, I would suspect," Bud answered guardedly.

"It's a 1989 Silver Spur. Kind of like the cafe here, one of a kind indeed. They only made a few over 6,000. It's on the same frame as a Silver Spirit."

"Very nice," Bud replied.

"It's really a luxury vehicle, maybe kind of out of place here in the sticks. Sure couldn't get in someplace like the Blue Castle with this."

Bud was now doubly wary. How did Bill know about the Blue Castle? Was he deliberately taunting him? On the other hand, the

Blue Castle was visible from most of Green River and no secret, kind of a well-known landmark, even though Howie hadn't known what it was called.

Bill continued, "It's really a classic, a very British car. It has its own personality. Kind of sounds like thunder when you start it up. Want to go for a ride sometime?"

Bud stepped back. He would love to go for a ride in this car, but visions of cement shoes now came into his mind.

He replied, "No, I mean, I would love to, but I need to get some lunch. Haven't eaten all morning and I'm a bit prone to weakness if I don't eat regularly."

"Well, I meant later, anyway, as Penny's gone and I can't leave right now," Bill answered. "It's pretty quiet, but someone may come along and want to eat. That's what these cafes are all about, you know."

They turned and went up the steps, opening the door, which had an ad for Desert Star Holdings, Inc., taped onto the glass, touting all the great things coming to Thompson Springs.

Below that was a Shakespeare in the Sagebrush flyer. Bud stopped to read it.

*What if Shakespeare had been born a few hundred years later and in the American West? Would he have hung out with Mark Twain? Come and see the New York Shakespeare Company's latest foray into a new and revised Shakespeare in their latest Out West production.*

Bud noted the dates, wondering if the actors would be able to pull it off. They were indeed running out of time, just as Howie had said.

Bud went on inside and sat down in a booth in the back.

"Mind if I join you?" Bill asked. "Penny's gone for a bit, and I need a break. I'll take your order and have some lunch with you. Our special today is Ciabatta fried-egg bun with bacon, avocado, and provolone. I'm trying to cater a little more to the local tastes, but if you prefer something more refined, I also have French onion soup garnished with Asiago Ciabatta croutons. And for the sanguine, I have red-velvet cupcakes for dessert. That's a little joke, by the way. Get it? Sanguine, red cupcakes...?"

Bud had no idea what Bill was talking about, but smiled anyway. Bill seemed fairly intellectual for a Mafioso, Bud mused.

"I'll try the soup with a cupcake on the side and a cup of coffee," Bud said.

"Beautiful combination. I'm going to have the same, minus the cupcake. I need to watch my weight a bit," Bill replied, heading for the kitchen.

Bud tried not to think about dieting, as it was a topic he preferred to ignore, even though Wilma Jean would bring it up once in awhile. He didn't see himself as being very overweight, but he knew he could stand to lose a few pounds, and all these gourmet cupcakes sure weren't helping things.

He looked around. There was no one else in the cafe, which didn't surprise Bud, given it was Thompson Springs. He was always surprised when he came through town and saw the cafe still open, as the town seemed to be slowly dying. The guy who'd bought the Desert Star had better hurry up and get things going, Bud thought.

Bill was soon back with their lunch. Bud was now wondering if he were doing the right thing, having lunch with a possible Mafioso, but he was hungry and tried not to think about it. Besides, Bill sure seemed like a nice guy, Mafia or not.

The soup was, as expected, truly the best French onion soup he'd ever had. He was so taken by it that he couldn't speak for a few minutes.

Bill watched him take a few bites, then said, "It's good, isn't it?"

"Delicious," Bud replied. "But how did you ever get into cooking? I mean, Howie thought you were maybe a prospector when he first saw you."

"What you're trying to say is, I don't look like a gourmet chef?"

Bud stumbled, "No, well, yeah, I guess you really don't look like someone people would say, 'Wow, there goes a chef.'"

Bill laughed. "It's been my profession for many years, though now I'm retired. I still enjoy it. I had my own restaurant in Scottsdale. But I sure don't care for this cafe. I'm about ready to take off. Just as soon as my gang arrives..."

Bud was suddenly wary again. "When is that?"

"Any day. One of them got hung up with some procedural problem, or they'd be here already."

"Procedural problem?"

"Oh, I have no idea what. They're always getting into something or other. They're all retired and have too much time on their hands."

Bud wondered how Bill could just go wherever he wanted when in the Witness Protection Program. It seemed like the law would have trouble keeping tabs on him.

Now Bill leaned over to Bud, as if not wanting anyone to hear, even though they were alone.

"Say, Bud, didn't you used to be sheriff?"

"I did," Bud replied somewhat cautiously.

"Well, I'm not one to stick my nose into other people's business, but you know the gal that's running this place, Penny? She and the owner of the hotel sure are thick. He's been gone up to Salt Lake, but he's back now, and I feel sorry for the poor guy."

"Why is that?" Bud was now eating the cupcake, trying to keep his mind on what Bill was saying rather than the subtle chocolate flavors.

"He seems like a nice guy, but he acts like he's flat broke, and he hits up every person that walks through these doors to buy into his investment scheme."

"He's not flat broke," Bud said without thinking, then caught himself.

"That director guy bought into it, didn't he?" Bill asked. "He seemed like someone who wouldn't be able to see a scam because he thinks he's too smart to ever get scammed. But I swear it smacks of something possibly illegal. I have a hunch Zack's never even heard of the SEC. Here he comes now."

Just then, a man walked into the cafe, Penny close behind. The guy couldn't be a day over 30, Bud thought, and he looked more like a poet than an entrepreneur, with his tortured scowl, dark eyes, and unruly hair.

Bill stood, then said, "By the way, I know you're wondering what my Rolls cost, as everyone does. I don't mind telling people what I paid—$18,000 on eBay."

He then added, "Watch out, you're next," nodding toward Zack.

# 34

Sure enough, the man who Bud took to be the same Zack Watson as in the ad for the Desert Star Holdings, Inc., was making a beeline straight for him.

But before he could get to Bud, the cafe door opened and three older guys came in. Bud recognized them as the same three he'd met before, the members of the Liar's Club.

One of the trio stopped as if assessing the scene, then said, "Zack, you might not want to try your fancy-schmancy sales talk on that fella." He pointed toward Bud. "He's an ex-lawman and might throw you in the hoosegow."

Zack looked irritated, then made an abrupt right turn and instead sat at the long counter, head down as if sulking.

Bud sighed, feeling a little like he'd dodged a bullet, the same feeling he got when he managed to see the local religious zealots at his door. He really would be surprised if Zack could sell anyone anything, though, other than maybe some tips on how to look like Heathcliffe—but then, he'd sold Greg four shares, and that wasn't anything to sniff at. Or had Penny had something to do with that?

Bud finished his coffee and left enough on the table to pay for his meal plus a tip, then headed back out to his FJ.

He had stopped at the cafe on his way to visit a spot in the back-country that he especially liked and hadn't seen for some time, the Sego Canyon Petroglyphs. They were just a few miles out of Thompson Springs, far enough from Green River that he doubted he'd see anyone he knew there. He wasn't feeling so gun shy anymore and now felt pretty sure nobody was following him.

For some reason, he felt drawn to go back to the area. Maybe it was because he'd first visited the place with his grandfather when he was a kid, and Bud was thinking of him a lot lately as he tried to figure out whether or not to take Hum up on his offer as a part-time deputy. He knew his grandpa would approve, having been a sheriff himself and well aware of how bored one can get when off duty.

But Bud's other grandfather had been a farmer down in Radium, and Bud remembered the peacefulness he'd always felt when spending time with him on the farm—it was where he'd gotten his love for plants and nature.

Bud drove across the railroad tracks and on through an even more decrepit part of Thompson Springs, heading straight for the Book-cliffs. The road was narrow but paved, and soon a spur took off and up across a small rise to Sego Canyon, where the abandoned ghost town of Sego sat, named by a coal miner who saw the name 'Sego' on a can of Sego Milk and liked it.

Bud stayed the course toward the Books, the road eventually turning into gravel as it narrowed even more, looking like it would soon dead-end at the massive sandstone cliffs ahead. But instead, a narrow canyon soon came into view—this was Thompson Canyon, and, interestingly enough, home to the Sego Canyon petroglyphs, which Bud always thought belonged in Sego Canyon, not Thompson Canyon. It seemed like someone had gotten their canyons mixed up.

A turnoff ended in a small parking area in front of a canyon wall that had a wooden fence protecting it, and Bud knew this was part of a fairly recent effort by the BLM to protect the petroglyph panels, which were extensive, gracing the canyon walls for some distance.

A deep wash cut through the canyon, blocking some of the numerous panels from easy access. It had been some time since Bud had been here, and the fences were new to him, as were several inter-pretive panels that attempted to explain who had made the figures and when.

Bud was of the mindset that no one really knew much about them, other than approximate dates from carbon dating, which put some of them, the Barrier style panels, at around 6,000 years old. Other styles displayed here were the Fremont, from about 600 to 1200 A.D., and the more recent Ute ones, which often had horses and bows and arrows.

Bud's favorites were the mysterious Barrier figures, which show-cased large triangular figures with spiral eyes and often held snakes and had dogs at their sides. Of course, the figures varied with the artist, but he enjoyed the dramatic effects these seemed to display.

He passed the parking lot, crossed a cattle guard, and stopped where the canyon opened up some. The easiest way to get to the panels, in his mind, was to just slip down into the wash and walk along until you came to whichever panel you wanted to view, then to climb back out and up in front of it.

Because the canyon drained from the Bookcliffs, which saw a lot more rain than most desert areas, the wash was able to sustain healthy stands of tall rabbitbrush and Fremont mahonia, also called desert holly, which made walking through the wash more difficult, but still doable.

Bud examined the panel closest to his FJ, which had some nice Barrier figures mixed with Fremont, then he carefully slipped down into the wash, mindful that the sun was setting and his viewing time was short.

It didn't really matter, as he was here more for the good memories than to study the rock art. He noted a few historic inscriptions, along with a few more recent ones. One read *Gay Whipple 1884*, another said, *Jesus G. 1926*, and another read, *R. loves J. 1987*.

The sun was now setting, casting a golden glow on the far canyon wall, and Bud leaned against the cool dirt along the wash bank, thinking of his two grandpas and how different their lives had been from one another.

He was now at a crossroads of a sort, having to choose between one or the other, being a lawman or a farmer, and it was a difficult decision, as both professions had their pluses and minuses. He thought he'd already made that decision when he'd quit his job as sheriff to work on the farm, yet here it was again. Apparently he was more conflicted than he thought.

But on the other hand, why was he making it into such a serious thing? Why couldn't he have the best of both by farming in the spring and summer and being a lawman in the winter? He could even take the autumns off and hang out with Wilma Jean.

He relaxed, deciding that maybe this wasn't such a life-altering decision after all. And as he leaned there against the bank and watched the sun light up the wispy distant clouds, turning them a soft pink, he felt that life was good. He wouldn't want to be anywhere else right now except in this wash with the desert holly and rock art and pink clouds and tall cliffs towering overhead.

Just then, he heard a car drive up. It appeared to be another yellow Jeep, and sure enough, it had the Cliff-Wrangler Jeep Rentals logo on the side, though this was just a two-door, unlike Greg's four-door.

It pulled up right next to where he was, though he knew they couldn't see him down in the wash. He groaned. So much for solitude.

A couple stepped out and came over next to the wooden fence, talking.

Bud leaned out a bit from behind the holly to take a look. He was surprised to see the couple was Lucy and Julian.

# 35

"These old paintings are kind of weird, don't you think? Anyway, what did you want to talk about?"

Bud recognized Lucy's voice.

Julian kind of grunted in agreement, then said, "Do you think the sheriff knows about you and Greg?"

Lucy replied, "What's to know, Julian? That we were close, in spite of his general obnoxiousness?"

"Well, I was thinking more along the lines of Greg being murdered."

"I had nothing to do with that."

Bud squirmed a little, then carefully ducked down behind a big stand of holly, making sure there was no way he could be seen. He really didn't like eavesdropping, but this was too interesting to ignore. Besides, he hadn't asked them to come out here and interrupt his peace and quiet by talking about something he was really interested in.

Julian said, "You were gone that evening, Lucy, and nobody knew where you were. I know, because I was worried and asked about you."

"Worried about me? Why?"

"You know, Greg. He was about to lose it. I worried he would take it out on you."

"He'd already lost it, if you ask me," Lucy replied.

"I know, he was a total failure as a director, and he should've stayed at Belham Castle, you and I know that, but do you really think everyone else thought that?"

Lucy now sounded angry. "Of course! Don't you remember about basically getting run out of town for our last production? It was ghastly. People hated it, and quite frankly, so did I. I know you did, too."

"I did. But Lucy, he could ruin his own career, I didn't care about that, but to ruin yours? You still considered him your friend after that?"

"I know, but he was pitiful. I worried about him trying to kill himself, especially after he realized he'd invested his last little chunk of change in a scam."

Julian asked, "How do you know it was a scam?"

"All you have to do is look around that little town to know that it's never going to amount to anything. If Greg hadn't been so greedy, he would've seen that. Instead, he sinks his whole life savings into it. He didn't even ask for a prospectus. I doubt if there is one."

"Don't you think it would be wise to go to the police?"

Lucy said, "Here? What police? There's nobody around to investigate. And what would I tell them, that a dead man got scammed? The plaintiff is dead, Julian, dead. Just like in that dreadful Scottish play where everyone's eventually dead. I told him we should never do that play, it's bad luck. He never listened to anyone."

Julian paused, then asked, "What about the sheriff?"

"Look, we're out in the middle of nowhere here, not in New York. They don't have detectives out here. The only one who might be able to figure anything out is Bud Shumway, and he's a melon farmer. That should tell you something."

"Lucy, you have to be straight up with me. What do you know about Greg's death? You were there, weren't you? I mean, look, I saw you guys go off together that afternoon. Next thing I know, you've called me to come pick you up way out in the boonies in the dark, and then I find out Greg's dead. I think you owe me an explanation."

"You would accuse me, your good friend, of murder? I'm totally insulted, Julian. Let's go."

Bud could hear Julian sigh. "No, I don't mean it that way, Lucy. Calm down. Look, I know you're a crack shot. I know all about your past. I'm not going to mention it to anyone..."

"How do you know about that?"

"When you first joined the troupe, I did a background search. Don't get mad, I do that to everyone. It's easy to find out you were on the college crack-shot pistol team. You almost made it to the Olympics. If anyone knows how to shoot a gun, you do, Lucy. And you have as good of a motive to kill him as anyone—he ruined your acting career."

"I'm done with this. Let's go. I'm totally insulted that you think I could kill Greg. We were close, Julian, you know that."

Julian sounded frustrated. "OK, I'm sorry. Maybe I'm just projecting, because there were plenty of times I sure as hellsbells could've killed the guy. He had lots of enemies."

"Look, Julian, I just want to go back to the hotel. Now!"

"I'm sorry, Luce. Let's be friends. Look, he hurt a lot of people."

Now Lucy seemed somewhat conciliatory. "I wasn't real fond of the guy myself sometimes, but to kill him, no, I would never go there. And if I did, I sure would never admit it to you or anyone else. I'm not stupid. Let's go back."

"I know, Luce, I know."

"It looks like it's going to rain."

"OK, let's go."

Bud leaned back against the edge of the bank, somewhat in shock, dirt crumbling down into his shirt.

He finally got up and walked up the wash until he came to his FJ in the dark. It was starting to sprinkle.

Driving home, his thoughts flipped back and forth like his windshield wipers, going nowhere in spite of lots of motion, wondering if he might now know who had shot at him that night out by the Blue Castle.

# 36

It was dawn, and Bud stood on the steep slopes of the Blue Castle.

A strong feeling of uncertainty had pulled him from his warm cozy bed, telling him the clues to Greg's murder were here and that he'd simply overlooked them before.

He had wandered around the wash where the yellow Jeep had been, looked around in the creosote some more, and even walked all the way down to where the little dirt two-track took off from Long Street, looking for more tracks, but he still hadn't found anything new. And yet, this feeling told him there was something here.

He now stood above the pour-over where the Jeep had been, a drop of about 30 feet. He was thinking of hanging it up and going home, but he would have to walk back around the other way to get down. He could see his FJ below him, just right there, but there was no way he could get to it.

Even though it was early, he was tired, so he sat down on the edge of the drop off, letting his feet dangle off. He would take a break, then go home and have some breakfast. For some reason, he'd come out here without even as much of a cup of coffee.

As he sat there, trying to think and put everything together, with no luck, he could hear an airplane coming over the Books, and it sounded like it was fairly low. Probably someone coming into the Green River Airport, he figured, wondering why they were out so early.

Sure enough, a bright yellow plane suddenly appeared over the high flanks of the nearby ridge, barely high enough to avoid the rocky turrets. Bud wondered if they might be having problems to be flying so low.

Now the plane appeared to be heading straight for the Blue Castle, and though the plane was still higher than the topmost rocks, Bud wondered why it would risk flying so close to the only danger in the valley, now that it had topped over the Books. Why not head straight for the airport?

As Bud watched, the plane came closer and closer, all the while losing altitude. It was either in trouble or was flying some kind of recon mission, as it was now just barely high enough to miss the rubbly point of the Blue Castle. It flew on over, so low that Bud could easily make out its tail number. It looked to be a Cessna 350.

Bud was relieved, as it now seemed to be headed for the airport, but it suddenly tipped its wings and flew back around in a tight circle, headed once again for the Blue Castle like a bug to a light. And Bud could now make out a blue beam coming from inside the cockpit. A laser! Why would a pilot carry a laser penlight? The beam seemed to be pointed right at him, as if trying to tell him something.

Bud nervously stood. The plane was coming right for him, as if it were now out of control, losing altitude rapidly. He couldn't believe his eyes. Why had the pilot turned around if he were having trouble, heading right for the only large monument in the valley when he'd previously been clear?

Now Bud was moving as fast he could across the slippery shale, trying to get around on the backside of the Blue Castle, as it looked like the plane was definitely going to crash into it. He was incredulous—what had been a peaceful quiet place to watch the morning dawn had now turned into a maelstrom of noise and fear. The plane was so close now that its engine was deafening.

Bud hit the ground, the wheels almost on his shoulder. Before he could even look up to see what had happened, he heard the terrible sound of metal crunching into rock, sounding like it had twisted and split into a million yellow pieces. He could now smell smoke, and his only thought was to get away as fast as he could, but instead, he rolled over and watched in horror.

The plane had indeed crashed into the side of the Blue Castle, and not more than 40 feet from him. Strangely enough, even though he had heard metal twisting and glass shattering and could smell smoke, the plane wasn't on fire and appeared to be intact, except for the fact that it was on its back, wings on the ground and wheels upside down, still turning.

And now, as Bud watched, the plane began sliding down the steep slope, blue shale sliding with it, heading straight for the pour-over where he had sat just a few minutes before with his feet dangling over the edge.

To Bud's amazement, as the plane slipped over the edge, it somehow managed to flip over and land on its wheels, righting itself. It seemed miraculous, and he could see the shock of the landing had flattened the tires.

Now Bud could barely make out the pilot inside, and he looked like he'd smashed his head on something, as Bud could make out a strange indentation in the guy's skull, even from where he was sitting. The pilot's head hung down onto his chest, and Bud was sure he must be dead.

He stood and rubbed his eyes in shock. He couldn't believe what he was seeing.

The pilot looked just like Greg Anderson!

But now, a strange sound was coming from inside the cockpit, a sound that gave Bud chills, as he knew Greg had to be dead, and yet he seemed to be making some kind of a whimpering noise, as if wanting Bud to help him.

Bud started crawling toward the plane, even though his instincts told him to run. But he now seemed to be in the control of some other force, some other being, and he had no choice but to do their bidding, to help them.

Suddenly, Bud woke in a cold sweat, Hoppie on the floor by the bed where he'd apparently fallen off, whining and whimpering, wanting Bud to help him back up.

Pierre was stretched out on Wilma Jean's pillow, sleeping, and Wilma Jean was in the kitchen making a pot of coffee.

There was no airplane in sight. It had all been a dream.

He rubbed his eyes, trying to wake up, then reached down and picked Hoppie up, dragging him back up onto the bed.

Wilma Jean had pulled the bedroom curtains back, not wanting to turn on the light and wake Bud up, and he could see it was barely dawn outside.

He got up and looked out the window—it had sprinkled a little last night, nothing serious, but dark clouds hid the sun and looked like they might open up any minute into a deluge.

He crawled back under the covers—it would be a good day to stay home for once.

# 37

Bud was still in bed by the time Wilma Jean was ready to go to the cafe, which was unusual for him, as he was typically an early riser. But he was still trying to process what had to have been a dream, as here he was, in bed and not out at the Blue Castle.

He felt relieved. The dream had been so real, and yet so surreal, and he was glad to know it was just his overactive brain and not something that had actually happened.

The dogs were now in the kitchen eating breakfast, and Bud was hoping his wife would be kind enough to bring him a cup of coffee, but no such luck, as he could now hear her big Lincoln Continental starting up in the drive, and she was soon gone. She must think he was still asleep, he figured.

As he lay there, trying to sort out the dream, something hit him—it was going to rain! It had already sprinkled a bit during the night, and a hard rain was forecast for today.

He was suddenly on his feet, getting dressed as fast as he could.

In a whirlwind, he poured himself a cup of coffee, added some cream, stuck a biscotti in his shirt pocket, slowed down enough to carefully put on his shoulder holster with his loaded Ruger in it, then was out the door, little Pierre so surprised that he forgot to grab onto Bud's pant leg.

Bud had experienced enough of these dreams to know they were his subconscious trying to tell him something, and he knew by now to listen.

He had obviously overlooked something out at the Blue Castle, and if he didn't get out there now, before it rained, he first of all wouldn't be able to get out there in the slippery clay at all, but secondly, any evidence he had missed was likely to be washed away, especially if it was in the form of tracks.

He thought he'd done a thorough job of looking the scene over, but his dream was telling him otherwise—there was something he'd missed. And now he had very little time to check it out again, as it looked like it would soon be pouring.

He was in the FJ, but had forgotten something, so raced back into the house, this time Pierre grabbing onto his pant leg and dragging along.

Bud ran back into the bedroom, where he found Wilma Jean's pink Canon pocket camera. This would work just fine, as his DSLR was too big to stick in his pocket, and he didn't want any encumbrances.

Gently shaking the growling dachshund off, Bud was soon outside and on his way to the Blue Castle, hoping the rain would hold off for a while. He was almost there when he pulled over on the edge of Long Street.

A distant memory came to his mind, a time he and a friend had hiked up the drainage between Battleship Butte and Blue Castle Butte, that large tongue of the Bookcliffs from which the Blue Castle had eroded.

They were looking for a way to scale Battleship Butte, which had been named by pioneer pilot Jim Hurst for its resemblance to a large battleship, turrets and all.

Bud recalled that they had walked quite a ways up the wash that was the drainage between the two buttes, and he recalled that a small two-track road had ended there. It was similar to the road he and Howie had driven up, but was on the opposite side of the Blue Castle.

Bud headed again down Long Street, now looking for where that same two-track came out. Sure enough, there it was, a faint road, and Bud slowly turned, easing the FJ across a small wash, then heading up the drainage between the two massive buttes.

When the road dropped a little, he suddenly could make out tracks ahead of him. He got out. The tracks were visible here only because the winds hadn't yet blown them away, as they set in a lower more-protected part of the wash. Bud took out Wilma Jean's camera and got a few close-up photos.

After he was satisfied with the quality of the photos, he got back into the FJ and drove on, his tracks obliterating the others.

Soon, the tracks disappeared, and shortly thereafter, Bud found himself at an impasse—the wash was now impossible to negotiate in a vehicle. It was the end of the road.

Bud was puzzled. Where had the other vehicle gone? The tracks had come in, but not out. He turned around, almost getting stuck in the soft dirt, then headed back the way he'd come.

Driving slowly, he scanned the side of the Blue Castle, looking for some way a vehicle could possibly climb up it. It looked impossible, as loose shales covered the steep slopes. Where had the vehicle gone? He knew it hadn't come back out the way it had gone in, and there was no other route.

Finally, Bud noticed a faint track going to his left. He turned onto it, thinking it must end under the steep slopes, but as he got nearer to the Blue Castle, he saw a small outcrop that the road went around.

He drove slowly, thinking he was going to come around and find someone there, though they must've been there for some time, given how faint the tracks were. But as he came around the outcrop, he saw nothing.

Bud now got out, locking his doors, making sure his Ruger was handy, and began following what was left of the tracks as they appeared to climb up through a small break in the steep slopes, turning and winding along a narrow shelf until they passed out of sight around the curve of the Blue Castle.

Whoever had driven this had way more guts than he had, Bud thought, climbing on foot and following the tracks. As he came around the curve, he could see he was now high above the same pour-over the Jeep had been found under.

The tracks appeared to go straight down the cliff and right over the dry waterfall, taking a good amount of the blue shale with them.

Bud now realized his dream made sense. Greg had somehow driven the yellow Jeep up this treacherous slope, around on this ledge, then right on over the cliff. That would explain why the Jeep was turned around—it had landed that way, miraculously upright, the impact probably killing Greg and also flattening the tires.

It was now starting to sprinkle, and Bud knew he had to leave or he'd get stuck. These soils turned to muck when wet, being a mixture of clays and volcanic ashes from long-ago eruptions—bentonite clay, it was called.

Bud turned to go, but took one last look, the rain now quickly turning into a drizzle.

He couldn't believe his eyes! There, pushed down into the dirt as if it had been dropped and accidentally run over, barely visible in the flat light, was a laser pointer.

And next to it was the faint imprint of a small cowboy boot with three little stars up near a squared toe, with the rest of the sole having a distinct grid pattern.

# 38

Bud was now back home, the dogs at his feet as he kicked back in his recliner, his laptop open. It was now pouring outside, and there was no way he could do anything at the farm, except maybe fix that PTO, but the part still hadn't come in.

He'd already put the tractor in Krider's big quonset hut, having seen the forecast and knowing they were in for a few days of rain. No point working on something wet just because he hadn't bothered to put it inside.

And now he didn't have much of anything to do except try to figure out the rest of his life, as well as who had killed Greg Anderson, and since he wasn't having much luck on the first, he decided to check out something that was bothering him about the latter.

Howie hadn't called for some time, and Bud figured he was probably busy on the play and with his regular day-to-day sheriff stuff, plus he knew tonight was the regular evening for the rehearsals of Howie and the Ramblin' Road Rangers. Besides, Howie seemed to be leaning more toward having Sheriff Hum as his mentor, which Bud had at first felt a little jealous of but was now seeing as a nice break.

Bud booted up his computer, then pulled down the web address of the place in New York, the Belham Castle. He once again studied the photos of people enjoying the various amenities offered by the resort, from sleigh rides to a giant heated pool to fine dining, wondering if he would ever get that far east.

The furthest east he'd ever been was when he and Wilma Jean had decided to go visit her great aunt over in Denver, and Bud had made a promise to himself at that time to never go any further east than Interstate 25, a promise he had since modified to never go further east than Glenwood Canyon.

Bud was kind of daydreaming now, thinking of how he and Wilma Jean had once gone on a junket to the town of Glenwood Springs and stayed at the Hotel Colorado. It had been a snowy trip, and they had really enjoyed one particular evening in the hot springs pool there—it had been a real treat to sit in the hot pool while big white snowflakes came down all around them. It was kind of magical, and even better, Bud had really enjoyed riding Amtrak over and back.

They'd been able to walk right from the train station to the hotel, and then to the hot springs, everything being right there. Bud could picture it now, and these people enjoying their vacations at Belham Castle reminded him of that and of how he needed to take his hardworking wife on another trip soon, maybe even back over to Colorado.

Bud suddenly stopped, looking closer at one of the photos. It was that same photo with a foreground of people laughing and having fun while doing some kind of wine toast, but it was what was in the background that caught his eye.

There, sitting among a group of people on a patio, was a face he thought he recognized. It couldn't be, he thought, but the resemblance was too much for chance.

He zoomed in and was sure he knew that face. He pressed Shift-Command-3 and took a screenshot of the zoomed-in photo, then tried to zoom in on that, but the resolution wasn't good enough, and it became fuzzy. Still, he was sure he knew that face.

He stood to go get another cup of coffee and clear his head a little when his phone rang. He could see from the caller ID that he was obviously wrong about Howie now calling Hum for advice instead of him.

"Yell-ow," he answered.

"Sheriff, that you?" Howie asked.

"Well, I'm not the sheriff, but it is indeed me, last I looked," Bud answered. "What's up?"

Howie paused, and Bud started humming the tune to Roger Miller's "Dang Me" under his breath.

Finally, Howie said, "I just got the lab report on that bullet and those casings we sent in. They're two different types. The bullet from Greg is from a .38 special, but the casings of whoever shot at you are from a .38 special +P. Do you know what that means?"

Bud answered, "Well, Howie, a .38 special +P is what some call a 'hot load.' It's overpressure ammo—has a higher chamber pressure and velocity. You shouldn't use this kind of ammo in older guns because the metal sometimes can't handle it, and you might have cylinder failure. It has a higher muzzle velocity and stopping power, so people use it primarily for self-defense. Since +P ammo also costs more, it's not used as much for target practice."

"Well, it looks like we can't do much to solve anything without a gun, Bud, can we? And not only that, we now need *two* guns."

"Not really, Howie. If you have the right kind of gun, you can shoot both types of bullet. But I think I know where we can get a gun, and it might just match what you have there. Just a hunch."

Howie asked, surprised, "Where?"

"Howie, call Judge Richter and see if you can get a search warrant for Lucy Wellington's room at the Desert Star Hotel. Tell him we think she may have the murder weapon, and to put that in the affadavit. Call me back when you get it, and we'll go over to Thompson. But not a word to anyone—we don't want to give Lucy a chance to hide anything. Not even Maureen, Howie."

"I know, Bud. I'm good at keeping secrets, it's my job. Just ask Hum. He told me a good one the other day."

"The one about someone over at Thompson being in the Witness Protection Program?"

"How'd you know that?"

"You told me."

"OK, Bud. I get the picture. Mum's the word. I'll call back later. I sure hope you have the right person. Lucy seems too nice to be someone who would carry a gun."

"Well, Howie, you can be nice and carry a gun. Just look at you —and me."

"I mean, she doesn't seem like the gun type. Do you think she had anything to do with Greg's murder? Man, we would lose our leading lady for the play if I have to arrest her, and that would be bad."

"I don't know, Howie. We'll just have to see how it all plays out. Give me a call."

"Roger, and 10-4."

Bud hung up, then he thought of how the kids had called Howie an Alt A type. He was going to try it and press Alt A, but he couldn't find an Alt key on his Mac.

He watched the rain for awhile, then kicked back in his chair, dogs in his lap, chewing on a toothpick and studying the zoomed-in photo from the Belham Castle, mulling over what Hum had said earlier about thinking outside the box.

# 39

It was the next day, and Bud woke, thinking it was early, but a look at the alarm clock said otherwise. It felt early because it was still almost dark outside, and he could hear the sound of rain coming down on the roof. He snuggled down under the covers—there was something about rainy days that made him want to stay warm and cozy and lazy.

He could hear Wilma Jean making coffee in the kitchen, getting ready to go to the cafe. He thought back to the previous evening—it was the first they'd had together for some time, as she was usually down at the bowling alley, but she'd had one of Krider's daughters come in so she could have the evening off.

They'd spent a quiet evening sitting in the living room together, talking about life and things, and Bud had finally approached her about the possibility of his going to Radium and working with Hum. To his surprise, she'd been supportive, but only under the condition that they rent a house, and she go with him.

It seemed Wilma Jean was getting burned out and had thoughts lately of selling one of her businesses, probably the cafe, as it took more of her time. But if she and Bud spent the winters in Radium, she thought maybe it would be possible to hire Maureen to run things and give Wilma Jean the break she needed.

Bud and Wilma Jean had once lived in Radium, and they still had lots of friends there, like Hum and Peggy Sue, and Wilma Jean was thinking it would be nice to have the time to socialize some, rather than working all the time. They could let Howie and Maureen stay in the bungalow through the winter, which Wilma Jean was sure they would want to do, as Maureen was always talking about how cramped their little apartment was.

It had been a really nice evening, and Bud felt much better now about things, knowing whatever he decided, his wife would back him up. The only other condition she'd put on the deal, other than renting a house, was that they take a month off and go stay in the little town of Redstone, Colorado, a charming village set high in the mountains, which was something Wilma Jean had always wanted to do. Bud had no problem with that—a little vacation would do them both good.

Bud turned over, again wanting to ask Wilma Jean if she would bring him a cup of coffee in bed, but he hated to press his luck, given she would probably rather be lounging around herself.

Hoppie was still in his usual place under the covers on Wilma Jean's side of the bed, but Pierre had managed to drag himself out from under the blankets and was now on Wilma Jean's down pillow, stretched out like a little prince, his long lean body the perfect length for the pillow. He looked like he was comfy, and Bud didn't have the heart to move him, even though he wouldn't mind having an extra pillow to lean on.

The reason he now wanted an extra pillow was because, bless her heart, his wife had just brought him coffee in bed. It was almost as if she'd heard him wishing, but Bud knew it was really because she knew him too well—and probably wanted something.

"Thanks, hon, that's really sweet of you," he said, holding the cup in one hand as he scooted himself up a little.

"Well, before you get any ideas that this is going to be a regular thing, let me just say I have an ulterior motive," she replied.

Bud took a sip of the best cup of coffee he'd ever had—it had a perfect flavor, no bitterness, and was very smooth.

Wilma Jean smiled. "Jamaican Blue Mountain. Isn't it good? But before you get to feeling too spoiled, I need you to get up and come help me jumpstart the car. I guess I left the lights on when I got home from the cafe yesterday."

Bud groaned. So much for lounging around in bed drinking coffee. He reluctantly got up and pulled a jacket over his Scooby-Doo pajamas and was out the door, carrying the jumper cables though the rain.

He drove the FJ around to the front of the big Lincoln and opened the hoods on both, attaching the cables. They soon had the car purring like a kitten.

Wilma Jean left, and Bud ran back inside, his pajamas now soaked. He had intended on going back to bed, but there was no point in that now, as he was wide awake and would have to get dressed in order to get dry, so he might as well stay up as opposed to going back to bed in his clothes.

Oh well, he sighed. The melons would love this nice slow drizzle, and he and the dogs would maybe fire up the gas fireplace and sit by it, doing as little as possible.

It was starting to feel a bit like early fall, and Bud knew what that meant—the melon harvest was coming up. Some of the melons were already setting their sugars and would be ready in a mere couple of weeks. He knew he should enjoy his free time while he had it.

He grabbed another cup of coffee and a biscotti and sat down with his laptop. There'd been something on his mind for awhile, and now that he had the time, he was going to check into it. He entered some keywords into his Internet search engine and began reading.

Introverts are not people who are shy, but rather are people who need a lot of time alone to recharge their batteries, while extroverts recharge by being around others. A true introvert can do just fine in social settings or in front of groups of people, but simply prefers being alone.

This sounded a bit like something he could identify with, Bud mused. He liked people, but usually preferred his own company—that way he knew what the general consensus was about his behavior. He continued reading.

> Introverts are often very intelligent people. In fact, studies show that the majority of gifted people are introverts, such as people like Einstein.

Bud was beginning to think he really might fit into this category.

The article now listed a dozen or so famous people, claiming they were all introverts. The list included Abe Lincoln, Roy Rogers, and Audrey Hepburn, then went on to say that many actors are actually introverts.

Bud decided he must not be an introvert after all, as the very thought of acting made him cringe. Maybe he was an extrovert—but wouldn't extroverts like acting? He was getting confused.

> Being an introvert can be difficult in a society that caters more to extroverts. For example, many introverts are slow to answer, making people think they aren't very bright. The truth is the opposite, as the introvert likes to take their time and consider all the possibilities before jumping into the fray.

Bud leaned back, thinking of Howie. This would certainly explain a lot, and he knew Howie was smart, even though others sometimes thought he was a little goofy. But reading this was giving him a new understanding of his friend, and he hoped to improve on his own impatient attitude about Howie taking his time to answer questions.

Just then, speak of the devil, Bud thought, as his phone rang.

"Yell-ow," Bud answered.

This time, there was no hesitation.

"Sheriff, I got the search warrant. Are you sure we want to go through with this?"

"I'm on my way," Bud replied.

# 40

Bud and Howie pulled up in front of the Desert Star Hotel, and Bud could see someone over at the cafe next door peeking out from behind the curtain, checking out the sheriff's vehicle. He noted that the two-door rental Jeep wasn't parked at the hotel, so he didn't expect they would see Julian and Lucy.

He opened the old wooden door with its embedded large silver metal star, and they walked to the counter. The only ones who appeared to be around were a couple of older guys playing chess in the corner, one who Bud knew was a member of the Liar's Club.

Howie walked over and looked down at the chess board with its black and white chess pieces, studying it, then said to the Liar's Club guy, "Watch out for that bishop."

He then walked over and rang a bell with a sign next to it that read, *Ring Bell for Service*. Soon, the same woman they'd met before, wearing exactly the same clothes and biker's do-rag, came from the back.

Howie said nothing, showing her the search warrant. She gave him a deadly look, then handed him a key and said, "Room 21, upstairs."

They trudged up the stairs and knocked on the door to Room 21, but no one answered. Bud noted it was right next door to Greg's room. Howie unlocked the door to Lucy's room and they went inside, putting on rubber gloves.

The room was tidy and neat with its tall windows open, even though it was raining, the long lace curtains blowing a bit with the breeze. They both started going through the drawers in the dresser and night stand, but found nothing other than the usual overnight items a woman would carry, things like *Extra Platinum Facial Creme*, dental floss, and some chocolate kisses.

Howie was now looking in the closet, and he took out Lucy's leopardskin pillbox hat and examined it, shaking his head. "Women wear the silliest things," he commented, carefully putting it back.

"It's a costume, Howie," Bud replied.

"I know, but somebody had to wear it at some point in time for it to be a costume for somebody else, right?"

Now Howie was rummaging around in the bottom of the closet. He held up a pair of lime-green boots.

"Look, Sheriff. Lucy's Annie Oakley boots."

Bud was soon examining them. "Howie, they look to be the right size as the prints we found, but they don't have any little stars on the sole."

Howie put them back, then rummaged around in the closet a bit more. He then held up another pair, made of black leather.

"Bingo, Sheriff."

Bud took them and turned them over.

"Look at these soles. Three little stars and a grid pattern. Look at this fancy lucky horseshoe decoration with the three-leaf clovers on the boot's sides, Howie—see where it says 'Lucky Star?' Howie, these are Tony Lama Lucky Star Boots. Nice find."

Bud set the boots by the door, then continued looking around. He now lifted the edge of the heavy mattress.

"Look under here while I hold this up," he said.

Howie stuck his head under the edge of the mattress, then reached in and pulled something out. He held it up to the window, whistling.

He said, "You know, Sheriff, if I were a burglar, the first place I'd always look would be under the mattress. Looks like we hit paydirt."

He held up a small pistol. It looked very fashionable with its stainless-steel barrel, trigger, and cylinder, black grip, and pink stock. Engraved on the barrel were the words, "Pink Lady."

Bud said, "Howie, that's made by Charter. Weighs less than a pound so is very popular with the gals. Wilma Jean was looking at a Lavender Lady, but she decided she doesn't like guns so never bought it. It's a .38 special—in fact, if you look closer, you should be able to tell if it's made for +P ammo. Look on the barrel."

"It is, Bud," Howie replied excitedly. "It says .38 +P. And it holds five shots."

Bud thought back on when he was being shot at. They'd found five casings.

"OK, Howie, I think we found what we're looking for. Let's make sure everything's like we found it."

Howie carefully placed the gun in a plastic baggie, then stuck it in his coat pocket. He picked up the boots, then carefully locked the door after they were back in the hall.

"By the way, Bud," Howie said. "I got the report back on the Jeep from the Utah State Bureau of Investigation. Nothing but Greg and Lucy's fingerprints, but they said they found blood on the steering wheel in a couple of places, which would be consistent with someone hitting their head really hard."

Bud replied, "Interesting."

Back downstairs, Howie handed the key back to the hotel care-taker, who spied the boots and acted like she was going to say some-thing, but didn't, though she still managed to give them a dirty look.

As they passed the old codger from the Liar's Club and his friend still playing chess, the old guy said to Howie, "Thanks for the warn-ing, Sheriff. Never saw that bishop coming. He would've slaughtered me. These youngsters will take advantage of us old-timers if you let them. Should be illegal."

The other guy, who looked like he was maybe all of five years younger than the first, said disgustedly, "Butterbean, that's cheating, and you know it."

"Ain't cheatin' at all. It's doin' someone a kind deed. But this game ain't goin' nowhere fast, and I can see a train wreck comin', so let's go get a burger."

As Bud and Howie left the hotel, they could see whoever was watching from the cafe window was still there, still watching, and though Bud wasn't certain, he thought he caught a glimpse of purple hair.

As they got into the Land Cruiser, Howie turned to Bud and said grimly, "Things don't look so good for Lucy, do they, Bud?"

Bud replied, "Too soon to tell, Howie. But wait awhile before you send that gun in to the lab. For some reason, I don't think it's the murder weapon."

Howie looked surprised and asked, "Are we still looking for a murderer? Wasn't Greg killed by the blow to the steering wheel?"

"Yes, but we still need to know who shot him. Even if they didn't actually kill him, they intended to."

Howie said nothing and drove off into the rain, the silver neon lights on the silver spur of the cafe sign flashing off and on, off and on, calling people to come in out of the weather and have a good cup of coffee in what Zack the marketer would call a very special desert oasis.

# 41

"You know, Bud," said Howie as the windshield wipers beat in rhythm, making Bud sleepy, "I need to get this murder solved so me and Maureen can get back on our band thing. We have a gig coming up in a month, and between this and the play, we're just not practicing like we should."

"I know, Howie. I need to get back and fix that PTO myself," Bud replied.

"What's a PTO?"

"Well, it stands for 'power take off,' but it's really just the shaft that attaches to whatever implement you're using and makes it work, gives it power."

"Oh. You got a broken one?"

"Yeah. But say, you been writing any new songs lately?"

"No, not really. Too busy. You know, Bud, the human mind is a wonderful thing. It starts working from when you're born..."

Howie swerved to miss a big puddle on the road, then continued, "...and it doesn't stop until you sit down to write a song."

"Pretty funny."

"Yeah, Roger Miller said that. He was one of the greats of all time."

"Agreed." Bud wondered if Howie had heard him humming *Dang Me* under his breath the other day.

They were almost back in Green River, and a band of pale blue sky opened to the west above the San Rafael Swell.

"Looks like the rain's going to let up," Bud said, pointing ahead.

"I hope so. We need to practice the play this afternoon."

"How's all that going? Did you ever find a director?"

"We did. We've adopted a new philosophy of equality for all. We're not going to have a director, and now that we've decided to switch plays, I don't think we need one, since everyone knows what to do."

"You're doing *Romeo and Juliet*?"

"Yeah, but the old way, not Greg's avant whatever way. We're going to make it like the real play, except I have a new role."

"What's that?" Bud asked, surprised.

"I'm the Dialect Coach."

"How does that work, Howie?"

"Well, see, we're going to make Shakespeare so the every-day Green Riverite can understand him. The actors are going to do the lines as if they lived in Green River. Like, instead of saying, 'Romeo, wherefore art thou?' the actor will say, 'Romeo, where the heck are you *now*, boy?'—stuff like that. I'm the Dialect Coach. I get to tell everyone how to say stuff so it sounds authentic."

"Wow, that sounds great. Are you going to make the deadline? It's coming up soon."

"We are, because everyone knows their lines already, and all we have to work on is this new style, and it's pretty easy to adapt, 'cause most everyone talks like that already anyway. And getting costumes is easy, because everyone's been going to the Green River Thrift Shop so they can dress the part, just like regular Green Riverites."

"I can't wait, Howie."

"It'll be cool. But Bud, is there any way we could wait and arrest Lucy after the play's over?"

Bud sighed. "Howie, you know the answer to that."

"Do you really think it was Lucy?"

"I don't know. I can't judge without all the facts. You might be a better one at that, since you know things I don't."

"Like who's in the Witness Protection Program?"

"Exactly," Bud answered.

"It's really a bummer that I can't tell you, Bud. You're more reliable than I am with stuff like that."

Bud was silent, then finally said, "It's OK, Howie. But I don't want to tell you who I suspect it might be, because you have that one piece of valuable info I don't, and I might throw your investigation off."

Howie continued, "You think it might be someone besides Lucy? Like maybe she was framed?"

"Are you saying Lucy's the one in the Witness Protection Program?"

"I didn't say that, Bud. But we both know there's someone else who's mighty suspicious, someone we knew from the git-go could be trouble. Someone who maybe tried to frame himself so he'd look innocent. And maybe, just maybe, he figured out it just wasn't going to work, the law in Green River is just too smart, so he decided to frame Lucy instead."

"Bill Birdsong?"

"Exactly."

"So, you're saying Bill's in the Witness Protection Program?"

Just then, Howie's phone rang.

"Sheriff Howie speaking."

There was a long pause, then Howie held his hand over the phone speaker and nervously whispered to Bud, "It's Lucy, and she says she's been robbed—someone stole her boots and gun. What should I tell her?"

Bud was surprised. If Lucy were guilty, would she call the sheriff to say someone had stolen the murder weapon? He wasn't sure how that would work.

He thought for a minute, then said, "Tell her you already know who the thief is. Tell her you're way ahead of her and have the stuff, but you need to keep it for evidence and will return it as soon as you can. It's all true."

Howie relayed the information to Lucy. His last words before hanging up were, "No, Lucy, I can't tell you who, but are you coming to practice today? OK, see you then."

With that, Howie hung up and pulled up in front of the Emery County Sheriff's Office, just as the rain stopped.

# 42

Bud sat in a booth at the Chow Down, sipping a hot cup of coffee while reading the Salt Lake paper. He used to be a regular patron of the little restaurant when he was sheriff, coming in every morning for coffee and donuts, but ever since he'd gone to work for Krider, he hadn't been coming in as often. And since Wilma Jean had started with the cupcake thing, he hadn't been coming in at all.

He was worried that the owner, Karen, would suspect him of mutiny and quit making donuts, and since Wilma Jean normally didn't bake for her breakfast patrons over at the Melon Rind, Bud had decided he needed to get in and say hello. He sure didn't want to jeopardize his sweets outlet.

The fact that he'd had to let his belt out a notch lately made him forego today's donuts, but Karen had told him she had a pan of fresh cornbread, so he'd had a piece of that instead.

It was the best cornbread he'd ever eaten, leading Bud to believe that Bill Birdsong was doing a little moonlighting at yet another of the town's eateries, but Karen had been too busy for Bud to ask.

As Bud sat there, not thinking of much of anything in particular, something struck him out of the blue. It was one of those things that made him wonder how his brain worked, when it worked at all, because it was so out of place with what he was doing and thinking.

For some reason, he was picturing when he and Howie had driven up to the Blue Castle and found Greg's yellow Jeep sitting there. Bud had somewhat of a photographic memory for such things, and he could see it in his mind. He wondered why it had taken so long for him to recognize what he'd been looking at.

He had asked Howie to stop and had then gotten out of the Land Cruiser, looking at the tracks going up the wash. He recalled what the tracks looked like, even their tread markings, and he especially remembered noting that the same tracks that went in had also come out. If he recalled correctly, he had even remarked to Howie that there was a set of tracks going in and back out that were made by the same vehicle.

What struck him now was how illogical it was, and yet at the time it had made sense. Of course, they didn't know that Greg's Jeep was sitting up the wash, and Bud had forgotten all about it in the ensuing excitement, but now it stuck out like a sore thumb.

He already knew the tracks couldn't have been made by Greg's Jeep. For one, the tread didn't match, and the Jeep hadn't come in that way at all, it had come around over the shaley cliffs of the Blue Castle. He had pictures he'd taken to prove it.

Someone had driven in shortly before he and Howie had arrived, and Bud's tracking skills had told him it had to be very shortly before. The tracks showed virtually no weathering at all, and there had been a breeze at the time, enough to blow some dust and debris into the tracks in short order.

Bud recalled noting this, thinking at the time that Greg's Jeep was ahead and the tracks were his. The fact that one set of tracks came back out didn't even register, he was so sidetracked by worrying about Julian's call saying Greg and Lucy were missing.

Some detective he made, he sighed, thinking it was probably for the best he was now a farmer. Karen came by and refilled his coffee cup, almost spilling coffee in his lap.

He looked out the window, pulling a toothpick from his pocket and slowly chewing on it, thinking. Someone had to have driven up to Greg's Jeep and left, just minutes before he and Howie showed up. Given the impact Greg had suffered from the nosedive the Jeep took off the cliff, the odds were very good that he was dead when whoever it was drove in.

Had someone expected to meet Greg, driven in and found him sitting in his Jeep, shot him, thinking he was still alive, and then driven back out? If so, whoever it was had to believe they had killed Greg, because no one knew the real cause of death except Bud, the coroner, and Howie.

Bud jumped up, left some change on the table, waved goodbye to Karen, then jumped into his FJ and drove straight to Howie's office. He was glad he'd had Howie stop and take some photos of the tracks, because he was going to need those now to prove if his hunch was correct or not.

Howie was sitting in Bud's old easy chair, feet up on his desk, reading a magazine, when Bud burst in through the door. Startled, Howie quickly put the magazine on the desk, kind of shuffling some papers on top of it, though Bud could still make out the words, *Lost Gold and Treasure.*

"It's OK, Howie, it's just me," Bud said, smiling, thinking of all the times he'd been sheriff and walked in on Howie reading old lost treasure magazines, except at that time the desk and chair had been Bud's.

"Nice to see you, Sheriff," Howie smiled. "I was just doing some research for when I retire and get to go out with my metal detector."

"I didn't know you had one," Bud said.

"I don't yet," Howie replied mournfully. "I keep putting out hints for Maureen, but the darn things are too expensive. Probably won't be able to get one until I retire, unless the band somehow hits it big, and the way we're not practicing, that's never gonna happen."

"Say, Howie, remember those photos you took of the tire tracks out at Blue Castle? Can I see them? Can you print one out for me?"

"You figure out who they belong to?"

"Not really, but I have some theories I want to check out."

Howie brought the photos up on his computer screen and soon had the best one printed out for Bud.

"Say, Bud?" Howie asked.

"Yeah?" Bud answered distractedly, thinking he might know exactly who the tires belonged to, as they were one of a kind, over-sized, for sand. Lots of people in Radium had tires like that, but around Green River, which was all clay, they were more a liability than a help, so few used them.

Howie continued, "You know that Bill Birdsong fellow?"

"Yeah?"

"Word has it that his gang's arriving today."

"Whose word would that be?"

"Maureen heard a rumor at the cafe."

"Well, those kinds of rumors are usually pretty accurate, if I recall. Wasn't that how you heard that the Minot Marauders were killers? If I remember right, they turned out to be pretty nice guys." Bud was referring to a previous rumor that had been proved way off base.

"OK, I know, I know. But what if she's right?"

"And?"

"Well, what if..."

"Howie, do you think they're part of the Mafia or something? I was thinking about that myself. I'm wondering if Bill isn't the one in the witness protection program. I know you can't say anything, but it's just something I've been wondering. But I now think that it might just be..."

But before he could continue, Bud was interrupted by Howie's phone ringing. After a few minutes, Bud could tell it was something serious from the look on Howie's face.

Howie quickly hung up. "That was Sug Bailey. He lives just down the road from there, and he says he can hear gunshots that sound like they're coming from the Silver Spur Cafe."

"Let's go," Bud said, grabbing the photo of the tracks and instinctively touching his Ruger in its shoulder holster.

"Foul play at the Silver Spur Cafe," Howie replied.

## 43

Howie was again dodging potholes on the old highway to Thompson Springs, Bud holding onto the grab bar for dear life.

"I know you're wondering why I didn't take the freeway," Howie said. "I figure if something's going on, someone's more likely to try to get away on the old highway than the freeway, thinking they can ditch everyone that way."

"Good thinking," Bud replied, nearly hitting his head on the Land Cruiser's ceiling. He knew it would do little good to tell Howie to slow down.

They were now to a place where a side road swung down from a hill and met the old highway, and Bud could see something coming along it, though it was still distant enough he wasn't sure what it was.

He had a suspicion it was Bucky the Mutant Bus, and as it approached, he could see he was correct. The side road went under the freeway and met up with the road to the old missile base. Bud figured the kids were on their way back into town.

He and Howie were past the turnoff before the bus reached it, and they kept going—they wanted to get to Thompson as quickly as possible. Gunshots were nothing to sneeze at, Bud figured.

Now Bud thought he could hear a siren in the distance. He figured it was on the freeway, maybe a state trooper chasing a speeder. Bud watched for it, as the freeway was only about a quarter-mile away.

And, as Bud watched, he saw what appeared to be a line of gray sedans like Bill Birdsong's Rolls Royce heading down the freeway toward Thompson Springs, all in a row. He counted to 15, then lost track—he could still hear the siren, but couldn't see any State Trooper.

"Howie, better call Hum and see if he knows what's going on," Bud said. "He may have a deputy in the vicinity of Thompson. Gunshots are always something of concern."

"No need to, Sheriff. Isn't that him coming up the road?" Howie pointed to what looked like a Radium County Sheriff's pickup coming way too fast down the old highway, its lights flashing and siren on. It appeared to be chasing a green pickup, which was going recklessly fast.

The green pickup was plowing right through the potholes, not even trying to miss them, while the following sheriff's pickup was deftly dodging them, slowing it down a bit. Howie pulled the Land Cruiser to the side of the road.

"Is your radio on channel 3?" Bud asked.

"Yup, it is," answered Howie. " I just switched it. You thinking we'll get a car-to-car transmission from that sheriff's vehicle?"

"I'm not sure they can radio while driving like that," Bud answered.

Just then, Howie's radio crackled.

"Emery County, need a 10-200. Copy."

Howie answered, excitedly, "Emery County 10-4, copy."

The two vehicles were getting closer and closer to Bud and Howie, and now Bud thought he recognized the green pickup from the parking lot of the Silver Spur Cafe.

Howie quickly looked at Bud, then at his *WWBD* bracelet, then back at Bud, silently asking what to do.

"Block the road, quick," Bud said. Howie pulled the Land Cruiser into the middle of the road, and he and Bud jumped out, ducking down behind it.

"A 10-200 means he wants a roadblock, Howie."

They both stood behind the Land Cruiser, guns pointing at the oncoming pickup, which didn't look like it was going to stop. Bud was sure it was going to plow right into them.

Now he started shooting at the pickup's front tires, but it veered at the last possible second, flying off into the borrow pit of the old highway, where it bounced so hard Bud thought it would wreck. It then managed to cut back onto the pavement and continue flying on down the road. Bud hadn't been able to get a glimpse of the driver.

"Crazy," Howie said as they jumped back into the Land Cruiser, quickly backing it out of the way of the sheriff's vehicle, which had now slowed down and pulled over next to them.

It was Sheriff Hum Stocks.

"Boys, we got a wanted felon ahead, armed and dangerous. Get on the horn to the State Patrol and see if they can set up a roadblock ahead. Follow me—I'm going to need backup." Hum then spun out, continuing the chase.

Now Howie and Bud were following behind Hum, dodging potholes. The green pickup was now well ahead of them, and Bud wasn't sure they would ever catch up to it. Howie had radioed the State Patrol, and they were on their way, but he had no idea where they were on their way from, whether it was near or far.

Howie was driving like a bat out of hell, dodging potholes, while Bud hung onto the grab bar for dear life.

Finally, Howie turned to Bud and said, "I knew that pothole practice would be good for something, Sheriff."

Bud nodded in agreement, trying again not to hit his head on the Land Cruiser's ceiling.

Now he could make out something in the far distance, something right smack in the middle of the road, something big and shiny, as if made of metallic silver.

It was Bucky the Mutant Bus, and it appeared to be sitting across the road.

## 44

Bud was perplexed. How did the kids know they needed a roadblock? Had the state patrol somehow alerted them? It didn't make sense, as no law-enforcement officer would ever use a civilian resource like that—it might endanger someone's life.

The green pickup now appeared to have slowed down some upon seeing the bus, but it soon became apparent that it wasn't going to stop. Bud could now see the kids as they jumped for cover behind the bus.

At the last possible second, just like before with the Land Cruiser, the pickup veered to its right, shooting off the bank of the old highway, flying into the desert scrub, where it bounced hard, looking like it was going to flip over for a moment, but then continued through the brush, whip-tailing and kicking up so much debris it soon disappeared into a cloud of dust.

Hum had stopped by the bus and jumped out. He quickly took cover behind it and pulled out his gun, aiming at the pickup, which had come to a small wash and was now stuck.

As the pickup sat motionless, dust settling all around it, Bud could hear more sirens, and two Utah State Trooper vehicles arrived on the other side of the bus.

Howie and Bud now pulled up and also hid behind the bus, next to Hum.

Sage peeked around the edge of the bus, looking scared, and whispered to Bud, "Dudes, you going to have a big gunfight and shoot up Bucky? Man, those windows would be hard to replace."

"You kids just keep your heads down, OK?" Bud replied. "How did you guys know we needed a road block, anyway?"

Sage replied, "We didn't, dude. We got high-centered." He then ducked down behind the bus.

The pickup was now deathly still, and Bud could see that whoever was inside was hunched over the steering wheel, motionless. Bud was shaken, having visions of another situation like Greg.

"I'm going to radio the ambulance," Howie said.

Hum said, "Cover me, guys. I'm going over there."

Bud drew his Ruger and pointed it directly at the green pickup. Hum nodded to Bud, then carefully inched out from behind the bus, running to the pickup while Bud covered him. There was no motion inside the pickup.

Next, the two troopers ran over to the truck, one on each side. They then inched up to the cab and looked inside, guns drawn.

"Shouldn't I be helping them?" Howie asked with concern.

Bud holstered his gun and replied, "Stay down, Howie. Those guys have lots more training than you do. They know exactly how to handle a situation like this."

The troopers now had the door open, and Hum was leaning into the driver's side. Bud could see he'd taken a gun from the person's hand, as the metal shone in the sun. The troopers were now reaching inside as if helping someone.

Bud could hear the sound of another siren coming, and an ambulance was soon in sight, two EMTs quickly next to the pickup. It didn't take long before they had loaded the person into the ambulance. Hum gave everyone a brief thanks and left, following the ambulance.

Bud was now standing by the green pickup, comparing the photo Howie had given him to the tire's tread. It was just as he suspected—a perfect match. He had an odd feeling in his stomach, and Hum's advice to think outside the box echoed in his thoughts.

When they'd unloaded the person in the pickup, he'd caught a glimpse of their hair, and it was the same purple as he'd seen in the sunset that evening he'd been out at the Blue Castle.

It had to be Penny.

The kids had now come out from behind the bus, looking shaken. The big skoolie had its front end on the highway and its back end hanging down a few feet over a side road that appeared to be washed out somewhat lower.

"How do you get high-centered on a paved highway?" Bud asked.

"Well," River replied, running his hands through his dreads. "We went out to the missile base, just like you told us, dude. That's a very interesting place—underground bunkers, huge towers falling down, and these things that look like railroad sidings."

"That's where they launched the missiles," Howie said. "They hauled them up there by rail from the building down the road where they assembled them."

Bud gave Howie a look, suspecting he was about to get side-tracked, then asked again, "But how did you get high-centered?"

River replied, "Oh yeah. Well, anyway, we decided to go into town and see if we could find some of those lights the sheriff here told us about."

"What lights?"

"Those blacklight things. They're like little flashlights, but they have a blacklight in them. You use them to hunt scorpions. He said they sell them at the grocery store."

Now Starshine took up the story. "We saw this side road and decided to see where it went, as it looked like it went up a hill where we'd be able to look out and see everything. It did—went right up by a big microwave tower—then it dropped down and went under the freeway and joined this old highway here. So we figured we could get into town this way."

River continued, "It was the joining part where we got high

centered. Sage was driving, and he came straight on it, and the dirt road's a lot lower than the highway, all washed out, as you can see."

Sage now stated the obvious, "We need help."

Bud nodded, surveying the situation. It looked to him like A-1 Desert Rescue would be needed, and he knew it would probably cost more than these kids could afford.

Howie was now putting his red traffic cones out, one on each side of the bus, fretting about someone running into it, even though the old highway rarely saw any traffic, as it had too many potholes.

And now the two state troopers, who had been looking through the green pickup, were examining the current high-centered state of the bus.

One said, "We're calling a wrecker to haul off that pickup as evidence. I bet we can get you out at the same time. I think the wrecker will be pretty reasonable, since you're not the main reason he's coming out."

The other trooper added, winking at Bud, "In the meantime, we need to see your license and run your plates. I heard a rumor that someone stole the plates off an old VW bus and put them on a school bus, just like this one."

Bud knew the trooper had been talking to Howie. Sage looked nervous, but Star wasn't phased a bit.

She said, "Oh, we fixed that problem, officer." She smiled at Blaze, who looked kind of scared, then added, "But you know, I think you guys need to get busy and do your duty a little more diligently."

The trooper looked surprised. "Why?"

Star continued. "You didn't give whoever was driving that pickup over there a ticket for passing a stopped school bus, and that's a very serious violation of the law."

Bud grinned just as the tow truck pulled up.

## 45

Bud sat on the edge of the old flagstone stage in the park, examining the stones. They were smooth and a reddish color that led him to believe they weren't from the area, but probably from Radium, somewhere in redrock country. A few had ripple marks from when they'd probably been the shoreline of some ancient sea.

As Bud sat there, he remembered coming here to Green River when he was a kid and his parents were still alive. They were square dancers, along with Bud's Aunt Rhoda and Uncle Chet, and they would all come and dance on Saturday nights while he and his cousins ran around in the park, playing shoot 'em up and doing things kids do.

One of those things was drinking 3.2 beer in the bushes, as Bud's older cousin Davy would always sneak over to the big cooler by the stage and sneak a can or two.

Since there were probably a half-dozen of them all drinking from the same can, he didn't recall ever feeling drunk, and it was the doing of the thing that mattered to them anyway. The fun was in doing something they weren't supposed to do.

Bud was now kind of transported back in time, thinking of the good old days, and he almost didn't notice Lucy Wellington walking by. They were getting ready to have play practice, and Bud had promised Wilma Jean and Howie he'd come and check it out, as it was just a couple of days to showtime, and they wanted some feedback.

Lucy was almost by him, looking down at the ground and appearing not to see him, when Bud said, "Hello, Lucy."

She startled, then said, "Hello, Mr. Shumway. You here to watch the rehearsal today?"

"I am," Bud answered. "Say, Lucy, you have a minute?"

Lucy turned. "What's up?"

"Lucy, I'm not a lawman, so please understand I'm just trying to figure out what happened to Greg. Would you mind answering a few questions to help set my mind at ease?"

"Sure, I don't mind, though I don't know much about it. But we don't have much time, as the play's about to start." Lucy started fidgeting, then added, "I don't have anything to hide."

"I don't think for a minute you had anything to do with it," Bud said. "But I have a feeling you know more about it than I do. Were you there with him out at the Blue Castle?"

Lucy looked surprised, like she hadn't expected him to know anything. She sat down, hesitated for some time, then finally said, "I was. But how did you know?"

"We have a cast of your footprints, Lucy. Can you tell me how he ended up in the cliffs?"

Lucy put her hands over her face, as if she didn't want Bud to see her reaction.

"My prints? How do you know they're mine?"

"We matched them to your boots, Lucy. Sheriff Howie and I were the ones that took your boots and gun. We had a search warrant."

Lucy stood, looking shocked. "A search warrant? You just came into my room like that? That's an imposition of my privacy."

"When you're looking at murder and have good reason to suspect someone, privacy becomes secondary to solving the crime. Like I said, Lucy, we had a warrant. Judges don't issue warrants unless there's good suspicion."

Lucy's face turned white and she looked like she was going to pass out. She sat back down.

"I thought you said I wasn't a suspect," she finally said.

"I have a feeling you won't be if you'll tell me about that evening out there with Greg. I'm sure you're with me on this one, Lucy, and want to see whoever tried to kill Greg brought to justice. Were you and him friends, or..."

"He was my cousin," Lucy replied. "The only people who would put up with people like Greg are relatives, and I was his closest relation, as he had no siblings. His parents are gone."

Bud was surprised. He hadn't even considered that the two might be related.

"What were you guys doing in Geneva at the Belham Castle?"

She looked at him in surprise. "You know all about us, don't you?"

"No, or I wouldn't be asking."

"We were doing a play there. They had hired the troupe to put on *Annie, Get Your Gun*. That's where I got my Annie Oakley costume. It was the one and only production we've ever done that people actually seemed to enjoy, and that was only because Greg didn't try to mess it up. We're from Geneva, and Greg's parents had been friends with the resort owner."

Bud replied, "So, what spurred Greg into driving out to the Blue Castle?"

Lucy was silent for awhile, as if she didn't want to talk about it, and Bud was beginning to think she'd decided not to talk at all when she answered, "Greg was stupid when it came to money. He was greedy. He was conned into thinking he'd make a fortune if he invested in that stupid hotel scam. He put everything he had into it."

She paused, then continued. "So, when I found out what he'd done, I read him the riot act. He decided I was right, and he wanted his money back. He told them he wanted it back or he was going to the Feds. We knew they hadn't registered anything with the Security Exchange Commission."

Lucy now leaned back and sighed. "We were stupid and thought they would be honest and return the funds. That guy there, the hotel owner, he seemed clueless, but not really a bad person. His partner, she told us she would meet us out by the Blue Castle because she would be in Green River anyway."

Lucy looked like she was about to cry. "Greg was like a little lamb when it comes to believing people. My first thought was, why do we have to meet them way out in the boonies? But I wasn't too worried, as I had my gun, and who would suspect someone would be willing to kill over something like that? I mean, kill someone for $40,000?"

"Who was Zack's partner?"

"I don't know. Someone there in Thompson. Anyway, Greg asked me to go along. I think he suspected something was up. So, we went out there, but there was nobody there, and Greg decided we'd turned too soon and come down the wrong side of the Blue Castle, so he decided to see if he could take a shortcut and get over to the other side."

She stopped for a minute, then continued. "That guy's never even driven a stick shift, as far as I know, yet alone a four-wheel drive. He ended up in this scary spot. I wanted him to back off it, but he was too scared and asked me to go get someone to come drive it down for him. He was up against the side of the butte, and the Jeep felt like it was going to start sliding off. I told him to get out, but he didn't."

"There was no cell signal there to call anyone, and so I climbed up higher to try to call Julian to come help. That's when I heard a crashing noise. I finally got a signal, but Julian didn't answer. And not long after, I heard the shot."

"A shot?" Bud asked.

"Yeah, a shot. Someone shot what sounded like a .38 special. I know my guns. I was now scared to death, so I hid in the rocks. Not too long after that, I heard a siren coming, and I just stayed hidden. I was terrified."

"Why didn't you come and flag them down? You knew it had to be the law or an ambulance."

"I also knew that whoever had fired that shot was still around. I didn't want to get shot."

"So what did you do then?"

"Well, everyone left, and it was finally dark enough that I figured I could sneak around the side of the butte and see if I could find the Jeep and maybe not be seen. I was kind of hoping Greg would still be where I'd left him, but I also somehow knew he wasn't after hearing that crash. It was late evening, the sun was setting, and I could see well enough to make my way. Sure enough, the Jeep was gone, and I almost threw up, knowing Greg had gone over the edge."

"I then heard what sounded like a pickup drive up and someone get out. They were there just a moment and left, so I carefully kept skirting around. It got kind of precarious, so I sat down for awhile. I was crying, but I finally pulled myself together and decided to walk back out and see if I could try calling Julian again."

"That was when I saw movement behind this rock. I knew it was whoever had fired the shot, but I didn't get a good look at them. I followed them for a bit, and when they came down off the cliffs, they hid in the brush. I was scared and upset, and I decided to shoot and scare them off. I didn't aim for them, just close. But when they shot back at me, I decided it was time to get out of there, and I ran until I finally got back to the road and called Julian, who came and got me. I wish I'd seen who it was, because I know it was who killed Greg."

Lucy obviously didn't realize Greg had died of a head injury, Bud thought. He could now see that the other members of the troupe were arriving, and Howie had just pulled up on the other side of the park.

Bud said, "Thanks for telling me all this, Lucy. It's going to help a lot with solving Greg's murder. But I don't think Greg was shot for the money, I think he was shot because someone thought he recognized them. Would you be willing to tell this to Sheriff Howie?"

Lucy paused, then answered, "I guess."

"Thanks. And I'm glad you only fired as a warning, or I wouldn't be here talking to you right now."

He stood to go, leaving Lucy sitting there, speechless.

# 46

Bud and Howie were sitting at a booth in the Silver Spur Cafe, waiting for Sheriff Hum to meet them. They had just ordered coffee from Jackson's niece, who was now running the cafe.

Howie had a valuable piece of evidence for the case against Penny, who was currently in the Radium County Jail, waiting for federal agents to come pick her up and return her to New York.

She had spent a couple of days in the Radium Hospital with a concussion from the chase. An armed guard had been with her so she wouldn't escape.

The cafe was now swamped with older gray-haired guys, all who looked well-heeled and who Bud suspected to be part of the golfing set. Outside, a line of old gray Rolls Royce Silver Spurs, just like Bill Birdsong's, took turns parking under the Silver Spur Cafe sign for their owners to get their photos taken.

A gray-haired fellow in the booth next to Howie and Bud was talking in a loud voice, and Bud couldn't help but listen in.

"Yeah, I used to work for old Bill myself in his Scottsdale restaurant. I was one of his VIP chefs."

Another gray-haired guy asked, "Oh? What was your specialty?"

"I was his chef de plonge."

"Really? What was that?"

"Head dishwasher."

The two laughed.

Bud now heard someone in another booth say, "This old cafe is kind of cool. Did you know that there was a movie called 'The Silver Spurs?' It came out in 1936. I went and saw it with my grandfather, years later. I think I was about six years old. Man, how time flies."

"What was it about?"

"I don't remember much, just that it was some kind of shoot-em-up Western with Buck Jones."

"Never heard of him."

"Not surprised."

"You gonna stick around for that Shakespeare thing over in Green River?"

"Yeah. Sounds like fun. How about you?"

Just then, Bud saw Hum drive up, park his pickup, then come to the door. Seeing Bud and Howie through the glass, he motioned for them to come outside.

"Howdy, boys," said Hum. "Too noisy in there, and no need for anyone to overhear things. I don't have much time, as there's a parade down in Radium I need to go help with in an hour. So, where's the antifreeze?"

Howie went and got it from the back of the Land Cruiser, putting it in the back of Hum's pickup.

"We probably won't need it, with Jackson's testimony and the toxicology reports, but I betcha anything that jug is covered with Penny's fingerprints. Nice save."

Hum nodded to Howie. "Who would've guessed you would pick up the stuff she used to poison Jackson? And probably the old guy, too, if we only knew. Too bad he was cremated and the ashes already spread."

"How in hellsbells did she get them to drink antifreeze?" Bud asked.

Hum answered, "Not so noticeable if you put it in a glass of something like Gatorade. Lemon-lime hides the color of the antifreeze, and the stuff's sweet—ethylene glycol—pretty close to sugar. Looks like a heart attack and kidney failure. The body metabolizes it, so it's hard to find after the fact."

"So, Jackson's doing better?" Howie asked.

"Once the doc figured out he'd been poisoned, he was able to treat him more effectively. But the poor guy almost died, and he's going to have long-term kidney damage. What finally tipped us off was the calcium oxalate in his kidneys which forms from oxalic acid, a major metabolic product of antifreeze. Given what Jackson told us, Penny's going to prison for a long time."

"So I take it she was the one in the Federal Witness Protection Program? And no, Hum, Howie didn't say a thing. I figured it out by myself. I thought for a long time it was someone else, a guy named Bill Birdsong, but at the end there, I was pretty sure it was her."

"How'd you know that, Bud?" Howie asked.

"Her tires matched the ones at Blue Castle. When I was out there waiting for Howie to come back with the ambulance, I saw her come back. Her reaction at seeing Greg made me think she was innocent, but I think she reacted like that because she'd shot him and was surprised to now see his head smashed. See, she'd been there before, when she shot him, and had come back to check, to make sure he was dead. She hadn't noticed he was already dead when she shot him."

"So, Bud, you're saying she shot Greg Anderson but didn't kill him?" Hum asked.

"Well, Hum, you have her gun. When you send it and the bullet from his body to the lab, I'm pretty sure they're going to find a match. A .38 bullet, a .38 gun, and I bet the striations in the barrel match the bullet perfectly. But the coroner says he was dead before she shot him, so I'm not sure how the court will deal with that. But seeing how she's on probation..."

"I thought we were thinking Lucy did that, Bud," Howie said, confused.

"Lucy was the one who shot at me, but in a sense it was in self-defense, and she wasn't actually aiming to hit me. I talked to her yesterday, and she's willing to testify and tell what she knows. But here's my theory about it all, and I think I'm right. You boys might as well get comfortable."

Hum and Howie both leaned against the pickup and nodded for Bud to go ahead.

"OK, Greg somehow knew Penny from the Belham Castle up in New York—or anyway, she thought he did. When I saw her face in the picture on the Internet, that's when the bells went off. Anyway, Penny was in the Witness Protection Program, the WPP, and typically such people have been involved in crime themselves, that's how they know so much and can serve as a witness. And usually it's something pretty bad for them to be offered protection. So, I think Penny recognized Greg and was paranoid that Greg knew who she was. That may be why she died her hair purple, though that would make her even more conspicuous, in my book."

Howie asked, "Did he know her?"

"I doubt it highly, as there would be no reason for them to know each other. But she just knew she had seen him somewhere and jumped to conclusions. So, she tried to kill him. She didn't want him to blow her cover. She may have even thought he was someone coming after her."

Bud continued, "But that's Greg, and we'll come back to that. There's still Jackson and the cafe owner. So, Penny came out here as part of the WPP, and she immediately got old Tommy Gunther to agree to give her the cafe when he passed on. She helped him do exactly that—pass on, that is—and was then furious to find he had died without a will."

Bud paused, chewing his toothpick, then added, "Well, come to find out, Jackson was Tommy's nephew and next of kin and would inherit the cafe, so she immediately got Jackson to marry her. Why she wanted that dang cafe so bad is beyond me, but I think it was part of a larger plan of some kind. Maybe she thought Thompson was going to become something, like Zack was telling everyone. Anyway, Jackson drank too much, and I don't think she had much of a problem getting him to marry her. I called the Radium Courthouse, and they confirmed they'd been married. Penny then promptly poisoned Jackson with antifreeze."

Hum said, "I think the fact that she'd been involved in murder before and gotten away with it must have made her pretty brazen."

Bud replied, "She was previously involved in murder? I suspected as much. Well, she'd met her neighbor, Zack, and seeing his plan to make money, she got involved with that, too. She may have been the one that talked Greg into investing, as she could be pretty slick. She wanted as much as she could get from him before she killed him, too. She planned it all out, then convinced Zack to let her into Bill's room to steal his bolo tie so she could frame Bill for Greg's murder, being careful to not get fingerprints on it."

"Do you think Zack's involved in all this?" Howie asked.

Bud answered, "I suspect that Zack has no idea about any of this, other than the hotel scheme. But I'm sure he'll be interrogated by the Feds when they hear all this, especially the SEC. OK, so Penny then got Greg to go out to the Blue Castle under the guise of returning his money, where she planned to murder him. But Greg turned on the wrong road and ended up getting himself in trouble up on a ledge in his Jeep. Lucy was there with him and went for help, while Greg freaked out and used his laser pointer to signal a plane going over-head. He then accidentally went over the edge."

"How?" Howie asked.

"Lucy said that Greg had never driven a stick shift, so he probably popped the clutch and sent the Jeep right over, hitting his head so hard it killed him. Those shales are really slippery."

Bud continued, "In the meantime, Lucy had climbed up high to get a phone signal, but she was on the opposite side of the Blue Castle and didn't know Greg had gone off. Penny had arrived on the other side of the Blue Castle to meet Greg, and the Jeep was now exactly where she'd told him to meet her. She came over and shot him, not realizing he was already dead, then put Bill Birdsong's bolo tie in his hand, not getting her fingerprints on it. She didn't notice Greg's head wound because she was on the opposite side."

"Lucy, who was up on the shales above, heard the shot and hid.

Penny left, not even knowing Lucy was around. Lucy then heard Howie's siren, and we arrived. We looked around, then Howie left me there, and that's when Penny came back. I was hidden, and saw her get out and check to make sure the bullet had killed Greg, but she panicked when she saw his head wound, probably thinking someone else was around. She then left again.

Lucy stayed hidden until she thought everyone was gone, but then she saw me in the shadows, and thinking I was the one who had shot Greg, came after me. She's a good enough shot that I have no doubt she could've shot me if she'd wanted. She just wanted to scare me off, as she was afraid she'd be next. When I shot back, she took off, hid for awhile, then called Julian to come get her."

Bud added, "I'm pretty sure the reason Penny came back was to make sure Greg was really dead. It's pretty common for murderers to do that."

Howie whistled. "Man, talk about complicated. Makes my head spin."

Hum said, "I'm going to contact the SEC about Zack, Bud. I have a feeling he's going to have to do some explaining, plus return that money."

Bud said, "Well, from what Lucy told me, she's Greg's next of kin."

The trio stood there awhile, then Hum said, "I need to get going. Lots to consider here. But Bud, you given any more thought to my offer? We sure could use a guy like you."

"I have, Hum, and I talked to Wilma Jean. She wants to spend a few weeks over in Colorado after the harvest, then we'll come down. November first OK?"

Hum looked pleased. "Of course."

Howie looked perplexed.

Bud explained, "Assuming Maureen wants to take over the cafe and bowling alley, Howie, you guys can come stay in our house for the winter, rent free as part of the deal while we go to Radium. Wilma Jean said she'd mentioned it to Maureen, who wanted to do it, but it doesn't sound like she's said anything to you yet."

Howie was excited. "Your house? The bungalow? Man, Tobie and Bodie would love that—so would we. That little apartment gets old."

"One last thing, Hum," Bud said. "Why was Penny in the WPP in the first place?"

Hum replied, "She was involved in a financial scam, one that resulted in several murders. The Feds told me they offered her immunity and the WPP if she would testify against the others involved. They were sent to prison and, for some reason, the Feds decided Thompson Springs would be a good place for her, maybe because it didn't offer her any handy way to commit fraud, or so they thought."

"Or so they thought," said Bud.

## 47

Bud pulled the John Deere tractor off to the side of the road, letting the three cars who'd been patiently following him go by.

He'd finally got the parts for the PTO and had spent the last day fixing the tractor and was now bringing the float down for the Shakespeare in the Sagebrush production of Romeo and Juliet. He was cutting things close, as the play started in an hour.

The float was important for two reasons—one, it helped advertise the town's Melon Days, and two, they needed it as a backdrop for the play.

He backed it in next to the stage, then unhooked it and parked the tractor back over behind the basketball court. He had planned on taking the tractor right back out to the farm, but he didn't want to miss any of the play, especially since he had a VIP seat right in the front row, next to Wilma Jean, Maureen, and Howie, none of who had yet arrived.

Bud had just seated himself and was getting comfy when a small gray-haired man accompanied by a tall well-dressed younger woman sat down behind him. Bud turned and could see it was Bill Birdsong.

Bud nodded his head, and Bill said, "Hey, Bud, I'd like you to

meet my daughter, Carrie Birdsong. She just got here from Scottsdale, just in time for the big production."

The woman smiled and said hello. Bill then went to talk to some
of his buddies who had just arrived. Bud was happy to see them,
knowing that Bill's entourage of Silver Spur aficionados would help
bolster the audience, as he wasn't sure how many Green Riverites
would show.

Bud turned to scan the audience and see who was there, thinking
he could see a guy in the back wearing a navy-blue Air Force
uniform, when Carrie Birdsong said, "I'm so happy Dad found this
little town. He's really been having fun here."

Bud, a little distracted, said something to the effect that Bill had
been a big boon to the quality of cooking in the area.

Carrie continued, "Ever since Mom passed away, Dad gets bored,
then he does these road trips. He used to be a really well-known chef
in Scottsdale. Anyway, he heads out for parts unknown, finds some
little town he likes, hangs around, then comes back home for awhile
until he gets bored again. We call him the Guerrilla Gourmet,
because he's like someone in guerrilla warfare, going around to cafes
and showing up unannounced, improving their menus. They never
know what hit them."

She laughed, then added, "He has all these collectible old-car
buddies who sometimes show up. They have a lot of fun. By the way,
he asked me to bring this for you and your wife—it's a really nice
bottle of Cabernet Sauvignon."

Bud nodded in approval and thanked her, feeling kind of
sheepish that he had actually wondered if Bill were in the Mafia or
not. He figured it would probably hold the record for one of his better
poor judgments.

Just then, he saw a bunch of kids sit down in the back—it was
Sage, River, Star, Blaze, and Raven. He nodded at them.

Before long, River and Sage were standing by him. River said,
"Dude, nice to see you. Come on back and sit with us if you want. No
point sitting here all alone."

Bud grinned and replied, "Well, you know, small fish swim in schools, but the great whale swims alone."

Sage let out a guffaw, then said, "Good one, dude, I'll have to remember that. By the way, Bucky's doing fine since the rescue. You and the state troopers are all real Alt A kinda dudes. But man, dude, what was all that craziness about, anyway?"

"I'll tell you after the play—it's too complicated for now," Bud answered. He could see some of the actors over at the side of the stage, getting ready.

Sage said, "OK, dude, but we're leaving right after this. The Rainbow Man Festival was a big bust. Nobody showed. Not one single person. Probably for the best, since Star had this bright idea to have a Marriage Proposal Flash Mob."

"What in the heck is that?" Bud asked.

"Dude, she wanted to get a bunch of people together to help her do something crazy—I have no idea what, but she's good at thinking up crazy stuff—then she was going to propose to someone in the middle of whatever this craziness was. Dude, I was personally glad it fell through, since I had this hunch I was going to be the dude who got proposed to." Sage laughed, then added, "That kind of stuff is scary."

River said, "By the way, this play's going to be great. We watched some of the rehearsal yesterday. It's pretty cool. OK, dude, see you later. Peace out."

Just then, Wilma Jean walked up, holding something. Bud instantly knew from the look on her face that he was in some kind of trouble.

She said, "Hon, what was one of my peacock glasses doing sitting on the float?"

"Beats me, are you sure it's yours?"

"Who else would have one of these around here? And look, the rim's cracked. It's a wonder it didn't fall off when you were bringing the float up here. You were using it, weren't you?"

"Hoppie did it," Bud said, ducking.

"I guess I'm going to have to hide everything I don't want

destroyed," she said in dismay. "And I'm going to need you for the reception after the play, so don't you dare run off. Bill's made several maple-pecan chiffon cakes with browned butter frosting. But guess what Lucy said I could have, assuming you guys give it back to her."

"Her gun?"

"How did you know? It's a Pink Lady."

"I know that gun all too well," Bud replied. "So, Annie's going to hang up her guns, eh? I'm not surprised. But I thought you didn't want a gun."

"Annie? Oh, you mean Annie Oakley. She's going to show me how to shoot it. That will make all the difference. I'm kind of half-afraid of them."

Wilma Jean handed Bud the glass, then said, "Take care of this, good care. The play's going to start soon. I'm the announcer." She hurried over to where the actors waited.

Just then, Howie and Maureen walked up.

"Afternoon, Sheriff," Howie said. "Say, you think we have time to run over to the office? I have something I want to show you."

Maureen smiled and sat down, giving Howie a knowing look.

Bud looked at his watch. "We have about 20 minutes, Howie. We'll have to hurry." He sat the glass down in the grass by his chair, next to the bottle of wine.

"Let's take the tractor," Howie said.

They were soon tooling down Main Street, Howie standing on the running board of the old John Deere. He saluted Old Man Green as the old guy drove by in his beat-up pickup, staring at them.

They pulled up in front of the sheriff's office, and Howie jumped off and unlocked the door. Going inside, Bud could see that there, in the corner, was a Bounty Hunter Quick Draw metal detector.

He whistled. "Man, that's really something, Howie. Hows come you to get that?"

"Maureen says since we're going to be staying in your house and not renting through the winter we can afford it. Ain't it nice? It will even tell you how deep to dig. I'm going to take it out to the old missile range and do some detecting, right after the play. You're welcome to come along."

"Well, maybe some other time, Howie," Bud replied. "I've been conscripted to help with the Meet the Actors reception. I'd rather go with you, but I owe Wilma Jean a favor—a big favor. Anyway, we'd better get back to the park. The Bard awaits."

"As does the Lost Dutchman Mine," Howie grinned.

They both walked out the door and on to better things.

———

I f you enjoyed this book, you'll also enjoy the next book in the Bud Shumway mystery series, *The Ice House Cafe.*

# ABOUT THE AUTHOR

Chinle Miller writes from southeastern Utah and western Colorado, where she spends most of her time wandering with her dogs. She has an A.S. in Geology, a B.A. in Anthropology and an M.A. in Linguistics.

If you enjoyed this book, you'll also enjoy the other books in the Bud Shumway mystery series:

*The Ghost Rock Cafe*
*The Slickrock Cafe*
*The Paradox Cafe*
*The No Delay Cafe*
*The Silver Spur Cafe* (This is the fifth book in the series.)
*The Ice House Cafe*
*The Rattlesnake Cafe*
*The Beartooth Cafe*
*The Melon Rind Cafe*
*The Cessna Cafe*
*The Klondike Cafe*
*The Yellow Cat Cafe*
*The Swiftcurrent Cafe*
*The Sunnyside Cafe*
*The Temple Mountain Cafe*

And don't miss *Desert Rats: Adventures in the American Outback, Uranium Daughter, Wandering off the Map,* and *The Impossibility of Loneliness,* also by Chinle Miller.

And if you enjoy Bigfoot stories, you'll love *Rusty Wilson's Bigfoot Campfire Stories* and his many other Bigfoot books, as well as his popular *Chasing After Bigfoot: My Search for North America's Most Elusive Creature*.

Other offerings from Yellow Cat Publishing include an RV series by RV expert Sunny Skye, which includes *Living the Simple RV Life, The Truth about the RV Life,* and *RVing with Pets*, as well as *Tales of a Campground Host*. And don't forget to check out the books by Sunny's friend, Bob Davidson: *On the Road with Joe* and *Any Road, USA*. And finally, you'll love Roger Dean Miller's comedy thriller, *Bombing Hoffman*.

www.ingramcontent.com/pod-product-compliance
Lightning Source LLC
Chambersburg PA
CBHW051649260626
47170CB00004B/1415